# THE WORKS OF
# GWERFUL MECHAIN

# THE WORKS OF GWERFUL MECHAIN

*edited and translated by*

## Katie Gramich

a *Broadview Anthology of British Literature* edition

General Editors,
The *Broadview Anthology of British Literature*:
Joseph Black, University of Massachusetts
Leonard Conolly, Trent University
Kate Flint, University of Southern California
Isobel Grundy, University of Alberta
Don LePan, Broadview Press
Roy Liuzza, University of Tennessee
Jerome J. McGann, University of Virginia
Anne Lake Prescott, Barnard College
Barry V. Qualls, Rutgers University
Claire Waters, University of California, Davis

broadview press

BROADVIEW PRESS – www.broadviewpress.com
Peterborough, Ontario, Canada

Founded in 1985, Broadview Press remains a wholly independent publishing house. Broadview's focus is on academic publishing; our titles are accessible to university and college students as well as scholars and general readers. With over 600 titles in print, Broadview has become a leading international publisher in the humanities, with world-wide distribution. Broadview is committed to environmentally responsible publishing and fair business practices.

The interior of this book is
printed on 100% recycled paper.

PERMANENT    100%

**Library and Archives Canada Cataloguing in Publication**

Gwerful Mechain, active 1462-1500
[Works]
    The works of Gwerful Mechain / edited and translated by Katie Gramich.

Includes bibliographical references.
Text in original Welsh and in English translation.
ISBN 978-1-55481-414-5 (softcover)

    I. Gramich, Katie, editor, translator  II. Title.
PB2273.G9A2 2018        891.6'6114        C2018-903330-4

*Broadview Press handles its own distribution in North America*
PO Box 1243, Peterborough, Ontario K9J 7H5, Canada
555 Riverwalk Parkway, Tonawanda, NY 14150, USA
Tel: (705) 743-8990; Fax: (705) 743-8353
email: customerservice@broadviewpress.com

Distribution is handled by Eurospan Group in the UK, Europe, Central Asia, Middle East, Africa, India, Southeast Asia, Central America, South America, and the Caribbean. Distribution is handled by Footprint Books in Australia and New Zealand.

Broadview Press acknowledges the financial support
of the Government of Canada for our publishing activities.

Canada

Developmental Editor: Jennifer McCue
Cover Design: Lisa Brawn
Design and Typeset: Eileen Eckert

PRINTED IN CANADA

# Contents

# Introduction

The Welsh bard has traditionally been regarded as male. Recuperative feminist scholarship, however, has in recent years done a great deal to challenge that traditional masculine image. When Catherine Brennan and I published a bilingual anthology of Welsh women poets in 2003, we set out to argue and demonstrate that the Welsh poetic tradition "is not, and never has been, exclusively male." The work of Gwerful Mechain is a key piece of evidence in this argument, for she is the only Welsh female poet from the late middle ages whose poems have survived as a substantial body of work. Her complex prosody and varied themes, her inventiveness and playfulness, and the dialogic nature of the poems' production attest to her position as a full participant in the mainstream poetic culture of her time. In the past few decades, the work of other Welsh medieval women poets has also been brought to light by a number of medievalists and feminist scholars, but Gwerful Mechain remains the female poet with the largest oeuvre still extant.[1]

Though our knowledge of Gwerful is limited, we do know at least a few facts about her life. Gwerful is mentioned as the daughter of Hywel Fychan from Mechain in Powys in NLW manuscript 3057D, which Ceridwen Lloyd-Morgan (following J. Gwenogfryn Evans) dates as before 1563.[2] This fact is supported by the evidence of Dafydd Llwyd's "Cywydd llateiaeth ... i Werful Mechain" (poem no. 21 below), which also identifies her as Hywel Fychan's daughter. The Welsh genealogies note that Hywel was from Llanfechain, and belonged to the Fychan (Vaughan) family of Llwydiarth.[3] Both places are in the county of Powys (formerly Montgomeryshire) in north-east Wales, not far from the border with England. Gwerful's mother was

---

[1] The scholarship of academics such as Dafydd Johnston, Marged Haycock, and Ceridwen Lloyd-Morgan has been pioneering in this field. More recent scholars such as Cathryn Charnell-White, Nerys Ann Howells, Gwen Saunders Jones, and Nia Mai Jenkins have continued the tradition of rediscovering the lost Welsh female poets of the past. My work is deeply indebted to theirs.

[2] See Ceridwen Lloyd-Morgan, "Gwerful, Ferch Rhagorol Fain: Golwg newydd ar Gwerful Mechain," *Ysgrifau Beirniadol*, XVI (1990) 84–96 (87).

[3] See Peter C. Bartrum, *Welsh Genealogies 1400–1500* (Aberystwyth: National Library of Wales, 1983).

named Gwenhwyfar, and she had at least three brothers and a sister. She herself married John ap Llywelyn Fychan, and she had at least one daughter, called Mawd. Her dates are somewhat uncertain but several sources agree that she lived from c. 1460 to c. 1502; what is certain is that she was a contemporary of the poets Dafydd Llwyd and Llywelyn ap Gutyn, with whom she exchanged poems (included below). There is some suggestion that she and Dafydd Llwyd were lovers; though he was considerably older than she, the poetic interchanges between them appear to give some support to that conjecture.

One of the most important characteristics of Gwerful's oeuvre is—ironically enough, given its sometimes highly unconventional subject matter—its conventionality. Her themes and techniques do not position her as a marginal or isolated figure, participating in some putative female sub-culture; on the contrary, she engages in poetic dialogues with her male contemporaries, using the same forms, metres, tropes, and vocabulary as they. She often speaks with a female voice and overtly sees things from a woman's point of view, taking her peers to task for their male arrogance, but she jousts with them verbally as their equal, confident in her own craft and opinions.

It is notable that Gwerful does not appear to have written in several of the conventional genres of her day; there are no praise poems to patrons, eulogies, or elegies among the poems by her that have survived. She may, of course, have written poems of this sort that are now lost to us. But as a married woman from a high-status family, it is probable that she enjoyed the freedom to write on whatever subjects she wished to; it seems quite likely that she avoided genres such as praise-poems simply because she was not obliged to "sing for her supper."

One of the most immediately striking characteristics of the poetry of Gwerful Mechain is the easy coexistence in her oeuvre (depleted as it is) of devotional and erotic works. In this connection it may be helpful to fill in some background; the medieval context is of obvious importance, but the religious history of Wales in more recent centuries is also of some relevance.

In the twenty-first century many Welsh people have distanced themselves from organized religion, but from the eighteenth century to the end of the twentieth the influence of Christian Nonconformity loomed large in Welsh culture; the past three centuries of Welsh history and culture have been largely shaped by that extraordinary efflorescence which was the Methodist movement of the eighteenth century, and by the "chapel culture" of a plethora of denominations in the late nineteeth century—among them Calvinistic Methodist, Independent, Baptist, Unitarian, and Quaker. In the wake of the notorious "Blue Books Report" of 1848 (a study of the state of education in Wales commissioned by the Westminster government, which alleged that the Welsh were poor, ignorant, and unchaste), indignant Welsh people took it upon themselves to display to the world that they were a people of the Book: moral, upright, and industrious. Though early Methodist religion had been expressed in the most impassioned and ecstatic way in the poems of hymn-writers such as Ann Griffiths (1776–1805), by the later nineteenth century Nonconformist religion came to be equated for many with a rather stuffy respectability and narrow-mindedness. Sexual prudery was part of the backlash against the allegations of the "Blue Books," and something of these feelings has lingered even into the twenty-first century. Even more so than for readers elsewhere, then, Gwerful Mechain's unabashed sexuality comes as a shock to the modern Welsh reader—particularly when it becomes clear that this openness about sexuality is not considered by the poet herself to be incompatible with religious devotion.

Much as it may surprise modern readers, some sorts of coexistence of the erotic and the religious is not entirely untypical of medieval literary production. Notably, the practice of collecting and copying various works into manuscript anthologies inevitably meant that works of very different genres would be found side by side. To take an example from a different linguistic culture, the sixteenth-century German *Ambraser Liederbuch*, copied by an anonymous scribe for Archduke Ferdinand of the Tyrol, contains songs of both erotic and religious content. That said, it is indeed unusual for such different sorts of work to be known to have been written by the same author; Gwerful's authorship both of playfully erotic poems about the female body and sexual desire and of utterly serious and sombre works about Christ's passion is, from any angle, quite striking. Other women writers of the fifteenth century in the British Isles, notably Julian of Norwich and Margery Kempe, were mystics who wrote of their visions and demonstrated their affective piety; though sexuality is present in their work and in the *vitae* of contemporary female saints and martyrs, it is almost invariably sublimated into religious experience. Gwerful's writing about sexuality and the body is quite different, and entirely unconnected with female mysticism. Its tone is frequently humorous and exudes an unmistakable *joie-de-vivre*: she is a celebratory poet in the widest sense of that word.

Some medieval women writers were forced to take up the pen in order to earn a living; Christine de Pizan (1364–c. 1430), for example, was widowed at an early age; it was as a widow that she wrote *Le livre de la cité des dames* (1405). It seems likely, however, that Welsh women poets of this period did not write for a living but rather for enjoyment; some have suggested that they had more freedom than many of their male counterparts in that they were not obliged to sing empty praises of their patrons in order to earn their daily bread.[1] Nor was the fifteenth-century Welsh female poet afflicted with the self-destructive dilemma of the later, nineteenth-century 'poetess' which Germaine Greer has eloquently described:

> The poetess accepts that she must display characteristics associated with femininity, such as delicacy, modesty, charm, domesticity, hypersensitivity and piety, as well as the filial, sororal, and maternal affections. What the poetess does not aspire to is the revelation of gut truths of womanhood, or any negative feelings of rage, contempt, protest, despair, or disbelief ... The poetess typically presents a sanitized version of herself; she and her poetry are deodorized, depilated and submissive ... The poetess's stride is encumbered by a train of esses.[2]

There is nothing "deodorized, depilated or submissive" about Gwerful Mechain. Arguably, it is her very lack of inhibition and her direct engagement with the "gut truths of womanhood" that has prevented most of her work from seeing the light of day until relatively recently. Gwerful's poetry, along with that of three of her male peers, was the subject of a University of Wales MA thesis by Leslie Harries as far back as 1933, but when he came to publish his research as a book twenty years later, he decided not to include her work along with the others. The reason for this strange decision can be found in the attitudes displayed in the thesis itself, where Harries states, for example:

---

1  See, for example, Ceridwen Lloyd-Morgan, "'Gwerful Ferch Ragorol Fain': Golwg Newydd ar Gwerful Mechain," *Ysgrifau Beirniadol* XVI (1990) pp. 84–96 and Cathryn Charnell-White, ed., *Beirdd Ceridwen: Blodeugerdd Barddas o Ganu Menywod hyd tua 1800* (Llandybïe: Barddas, 2005).

2  Germaine Greer, *Slip-shod Sibyls: Recognition, Rejection and the Woman Poet* (London: Viking Penguin, 1995) pp. xv–xvi; p. 37.

*Y peth pwysicaf i'w gofio wrth feirniadu barddoniaeth Gwerful Mechain, yn enwedig ei chaneuon aflendid, yw na ddylid ei barnu yng ngoleuni egwyddorion moesol y ganrif hon. Tueddiadau ac egwyddorion ei hoes hi ei hunan a benderfyna safon ei gwaith. Yng ngoleuni yr ugeinfed ganrif nid yw Gwerful Mechain namyn putain, ond yn ei chanrif ei hun yr oedd canu caneuon aflan yn beth cyffredin bron, yn enwedig ar y Cyfandir.*[1]

(The most important thing to remember in evaluating the poetry of Gwerful Mechain, especially her pornographic songs, is that she should not be judged in the light of the moral principles of this century. The tendencies and principles of her own age are those which determine the standard of her work. In the light of the twentieth century, Gwerful Mechain is nothing more than a whore, but in her own century singing dirty songs was more or less a common thing to do, especially on the Continent.)

Harries's characterization of Gwerful as a 'whore' (*putain*) is particularly shocking but the attitudes displayed here may be regarded as typical of that conservative Welsh Nonconformist culture developed in the later nineteenth century. It is also interesting that Harries attempts to characterize erotic poetry as a foreign, perhaps essentially French, genre, thus conserving Wales's image as the pure "land of the white gloves" (*gwlad y menig gwynion*).[2]

Despite his own prejudices, Leslie Harries carried out extremely valuable work in preparing scholarly editions of a range of Gwerful Mechain's poetry. The task is challenging because her poems—there are fourteen extant poems which are definitely by her, five which are probably hers, and a number of other anonymous works which may be hers—appear in many different manuscript versions. This, in itself, as Ceridwen Lloyd-Morgan has pointed out, is testimony to the popularity of Gwerful Mechain's work: her 'cywydd' to Jesus Christ, for instance, is found in no fewer than 68 different manuscripts.[3]

---

1   Leslie Harries, *Barddoniaeth Huw Cae Llwyd, Ieuan ap Huw Cae Llwyd, Ieuan Dyfi, a Gwerful Mechain* (MA thesis, University College of Wales, Swansea, 1933) p. 26. English translation follows.

2   *Gwlad y menig gwynion* is a term used to describe Wales, particularly in the later nineteenth century. It suggests a land of moral purity where the judges in court don white gloves to indicate that no crime has been committed. (This is in contrast with the wearing of the black cap to indicate the death penalty.)

3   Ceridwen Lloyd-Morgan, "'Gwerful Ferch Ragorol Fain': Golwg Newydd ar Gwerful Mechain," *Ysgrifau Beirniadol* XVI (1990) pp. 84–96. For a description of the *cywydd* form, see below.

Also notable is the fact that her poetry seems to have been known and admired by later Welsh women poets, as indicated by its appearance in manuscript compilations such as the "Red Book" of Angharad James (1677–1749). In this context, it is important to acknowledge that there existed in Wales alongside the relatively erudite strict-metre poetic tradition an oral, popular tradition of song, consisting of "*hen benillion*" (old verses) of anonymous authorship. Some critics believe that the anonymous authors of these lyrical verses—often very simple and proverbial in style, and dealing with elemental human passions and experiences—were predominantly women. Certainly the oral tradition has proved influential on the work of a number of later Welsh female poets, from the eighteenth-century hymn-writer, Ann Griffiths, through to the present. It may even be that the alleged laxness to which Leslie Harries and Nerys Ann Howells have drawn attention in the strict-metre verse of Gwerful Mechain can be seen to derive from the influence of the folk verse traditions upon her. She is taken to task by Harries for "not keeping to the rules very carefully." He shakes his head in despair over Gwerful's ineptitude: "*Deuthum ar draws nifer o wallau cynganeddol a beiau gwaharddedig*"[1] (I came across a number of mistakes in the cynghanedd and prohibited faults).

What Harries does not consider is that Gwerful may not have been particularly concerned to keep carefully to the rules; it is surely possible that she adopted an attitude to composition analogous to that of the composers of the anonymous verses which were passed on orally from generation to generation. That Gwerful Mechain's own poetry was often preserved in this way is suggested by Harries, who concludes from his struggle to produce scholarly editions of her poems from the manuscript sources that "the copies were frequently written down from memory and that they had been corrupted by those who copied them, or those who recited them" (*bod y copïau'n fynych wedi eu codi oddi ar gof a'u llygru gan y rhai a'u copïai, neu a'u hadroddai*).

Welsh women's poetry (in both Welsh and English, from the seventeenth century onwards) tended to circulate in manuscript copies and orally. It was not until 1850 that the first fully-fledged volume of Welsh poetry by a woman, namely *Telyn Egryn*,[2] was published. The National Library of Wales contains a wealth of hand written books of

---

1 Leslie Harries, op. cit. p. 25. "Cynghanedd" is briefly explained below.
2 *Telyn Egryn*, new edition by Ceridwen Lloyd-Morgan and Kathryn Hughes (Dinas Powys: Honno, 1998).

poems belonging to women—personal anthologies, really—mainly dating from the eighteenth century and containing the work of a wide range of female and male poets. Women poets themselves, such as Angharad James and her sister, Margaret Davies, kept such books; only a fraction of this neglected manuscript material has so far appeared in print.

Fortunately, a scholarly edition of the work of Gwerful Mechain did finally appear in 2001—Nerys Ann Howells' *Gwaith Gwerful Mechain ac Eraill*[1] (The Work of Gwerful Mechain and Others)—an edition to which the present work is deeply indebted. Even the title of Howells' valuable work was a neat riposte to Leslie Harries's *Gwaith Huw Cae Llwyd Ac Eraill* (*The Work of Huw cae Llwyd And Others*); Gwerful Mechain was, in 1933, among the Others, but in 2001 she took pride of place. One interesting observation made by Howells in her introduction is that the so-called "faults" in the cynghanedd of Gwerful's verse are not observable in her poem to Jesus Christ—the evidently very popular work found in many manuscripts and characterised by its sincere devotion and piety. On the other hand, Gwerful's erotic verse is full of such "faults," suggesting that when she wished to write conventionally and "correctly," she was perfectly able to do so, and when she did not wish to, she enthusiastically broke the rules.

In the cywydd to the female genitals, which I've translated as "To the vagina," there are large numbers of unconventionalities in the strict metre form, especially lines known as *"cynganeddion sain bengoll."* Cynghanedd sain is a type of line with an internal rhyme; it requires a full alliterative correspondence between the second rhyming word and the last part of the line, which Gwerful's verse frequently lacks. The result in her version of the form is a much looser, more fluid and racy kind of verse. Given that scholarship suggests these poems were frequently composed in an improvisatory way in competition with other bards who were also close friends—much like the *Talwrn y Beirdd* competition in modern times—it seems likely that the poems bear the mark of this oral composition. This idea is supported by Nerys Ann Howells' suggestion that there are strong similarities in voice, tone, and technique between the poems of Gwerful and the male poet with whom we know she was close friends, Dafydd Llwyd

---

1   Nerys Ann Howells, *Gwaith Gwerful Mechain ac Eraill* (Aberystwyth: Canolfan Uwchefrydiau Cymreig a Cheltaidd Prifysgol Cymru, 2001).

of Mathafarn. These two poets both take liberties with cynghanedd and end up creating a kind of humorous private discourse, strongly reminiscent of their speaking voices.

Many of Gwerful's poems are preserved in manuscripts dating from long after her own lifetime, indicating that her poems were often memorised and transmitted orally. It is probable that many of her poems have been lost; as it is, a number of her works exist in only one manuscript copy. Moreover, in the instances where many manuscript copies of the same poems have survived (as is the case with 'Dioddefaint Crist'/Christ's Passion, no. 1 below) there are many variations and inconsistencies among the versions of the poem found in the different manuscripts. About 40 poems are ascribed to Gwerful Mechain in the manuscripts but a number of these are certainly misattributions. I have followed Nerys Ann Howells in her standard edition who suggests that fourteen poems are indisputably by Gwerful and five others are probably hers, although I admit that this is erring on the side of caution. Since it is impossible to date the extant poems, they are arranged thus below:

1. Religious
2. Erotic
3. Dialogic
4. Englynion
5. Uncertain authorship
6. Contextual poems

Gwerful writes in two principal forms: the *cywydd* and the *englyn*. The *cywydd* is a poem consisting of seven-syllable rhyming couplets and is usually between 40 and 80 lines in length. Each line in this strict-metre form must contain one of the variations of *cynghanedd*, which involves a complex patterning of alliteration and/or internal rhyme. In addition, the lines must end with an alternating stressed and unstressed syllable. The great fourteenth-century poet, Dafydd ap Gwilym, had excelled in the *cywydd* form, using it to write love poems, eulogies, and satires. Gwerful is in many ways following Dafydd's example but she is also adapting the form to her own purposes. An important characteristic of the form is "*dyfalu*"; the poet uses her ingenuity to describe an object in a series of inventive ways, in a multiple and cumulative comparison. *Dyfalu* can be seen in Gwerful's poem to the vagina; it is a common device among medieval poets, who use it to display their inventiveness and skill. A more problematic characteristic for the translator is the "*sangiad*," which is a kind of aside, parenthetical statement or exclamation, usually taking up half a line, and which is often inserted in order to achieve the desired *cynghanedd* pattern. "*Cymeriad*" is an anaphora, in which the same word or phrase is repeated at the opening of successive lines of verse.

In comparison with the more stately iambic pentameter characteristic of much traditional English verse, the brief 7-syllable lines of the *cywydd* are lithe and agile, meaning that the form is suited to many purposes, such as telling a story, expressing love or grief, or light-hearted satire. The fact that the *cywydd* is constructed from couplets also means that there is scope for succinct and memorable, epigrammatic expression.

The *englyn* is a 4-line verse form which remains one of the most popular types of strict metre verse to this day. Its brevity means that it is suited to epitaphs and also to witty squibs. Each line in an englyn must be in *cynghanedd* and the most common form, the "*englyn unodl union*," usually rhymes aaaa. The peculiarity of this form is that the end-rhyme in the first line actually occurs three-quarters of the way through the line; there is then a caesura and a word which alliterates with the word(s) at the beginning of the second line. Gwerful shows her mastery of this form and her awareness of its malleability in her poem on getting her petticoat wet (no. 12 below) and in the savage curse on the husband who beats her (no. 11). These *englynion*, though they are in strict metre, are reminiscent of folk poetry in their domestic and vernacular tone. Although it is not possible to be sure that they are autobiographical, they do give the modern reader a tantalising glimpse of everyday life for a woman in rural Wales in the late fifteenth century.

*Cynghanedd* (Consonance, or Harmony) is characterstic of both the *cywydd* and the *englyn*. It is a complex metrical system characteristic of traditional Welsh language verse. The presence of "*cynghanedd*" marks a poem out as a so-called "strict metre" work, rather than an example of free verse. There are four main types of "*cynghanedd*" (with a number of sub-types): 1. *Groes* 2. *Draws* 3. *Sain* 4. *Lusg*. In the first two types, the poetic line is divided in two and the consonants in the first half are repeated in the same order in the second half. In "Groes" all the consonants need to be repeated, whereas in "Draws" only the consonants at the beginning and end of the line are the same, skipping over a section in the middle. The "Sain" and "Lusg" types involve internal rhyme: "Sain" combines rhyme with consonantal echoing, whereas "Lusg" contains only an internal rhyme.[1]

Gwerful is likely to have learned to write strict-metre poetry, which is a demanding craft, from an older, established, probably male poet. Often, the craft was passed from father to son; Gwerful may have learned from an older relative or, indeed, from Dafydd Llwyd, the older poet with whom she exchanges poems, and whose style she often echoes. Her extant oeuvre reveals that she was an adept crafts-woman, acutely aware of literary traditions, and able to adapt them to her own advantage. Although, as mentioned above, she has been criti-cized for the laxness of some of her work, the evidence suggests that she broke the established rules of *cynghanedd* only when she wished to do so, and often to interesting effect. Her lines are occasionally a syllable too long, as Nerys Howells has pointed out, though in read-ing them aloud this "fault" is not noticeable. Howells also notes that Gwerful's work is more lax in the humorous and erotic poems, while in the religious poems, perhaps because of the serious subjects, she uphold the rules of cynghanedd quite rigorously.[2]

The two religious poems by Gwerful that have survived are more conventional than her secular and erotic poems. They are written with an acute awareness of the seriousness and importance of the subject matter: Christ's suffering, and death and judgement, respec-tively. "Christ's Passion," to judge by the many manuscript copies that survive, was enduringly popular and one can understand why: it recounts the story of Christ's passion in a succinct, dramatic, and emotionally touching way. The allusions are all biblical and would have been familiar to a fifteenth-century audience; elsewhere, Gwer-ful is capable of showing off her erudition, but here she deliberately confines herself to the familiar New Testament story. The poem ends on a note of consolation and comfort, promising God's grace and pardon to those who seek it. Much less comforting and, judging from the extant manuscript copies, less popular, is the more admonitory "Death and Judgement." The poem has a slightly more erudite tone,

---

1   For a good explanation of strict metre, see the Introduction to Tony Conran's *Welsh Verse* (Bridgend: Poetry Wales Press, 1986).
2   See Nerys Ann Howells, Introduction, *Gwaith Gwerful Mechain ac Eraill* (Aberystwyth: Canolfan Uwchefrydiau Cymreig a Cheltaidd Prifysgol Cymru, 2001) pp. 23–24.

in that it offers a series of exempla from the Old Testament; while it also ends on a hopeful note, the overall tone is much more sombre.

The erotic poems could not be more different in tone. They are playful and humorous, though they undoubtedly have a serious feminist undertone and purpose. The poem "Cywydd y cedor" which I translate as "To the vagina" is Gwerful's most notorious poem, and yet it is still not widely known, partly for the cultural reasons mentioned above, partly because translations of it are not widely available. What is striking is the boldness of the voice and the ingenuity of the imagery, as well as the apparent ease of the metrical craft. It may strike a contemporary reader encountering it for the first time as surprisingly modern. Its candour, humour, and spirit of celebration are reminiscent of aspects of French feminist theory in the late twentieth century,[1] while contemporary women poets such as Sharon Olds are writing in a very similar vein today—Olds' 2016 volume *Odes*, for example, contains Odes to the Clitoris, the Penis, the Hymen, and Menstrual Blood.[2] Reviews of Olds' work, though mainly positive, show that these subjects are still to some extent taboo; as the reviewer Kate Kellaway puts it, "She never censors herself: her subjects are those poetry ignores."[3] This was, of course, Gwerful Mechain's complaint back in the fifteenth century: the poets ignored this subject and so she took up the challenge to write about it. It is refreshing to hear such a bold and uncensored voice speaking to us from over five hundred years ago.

The poem "To jealous wives" is in the same vein but less straightforwardly feminist. The female speaker appears to take to task those wives who jealously guard their husbands and refuse to allow other women to share their sexual favours. Clearly, this is a comic poem, and there are moments of almost surreal grotesquerie, such as when the husband's penis seems to be an object curiously detached from the rest of his body and to become a precious object possessed in secret by his wife. Like "To the vagina," the poem can be seen as a defiant rejoinder to male poets of the time, who often attacked impotent, jealous husbands—and often wrote misogynistically of the supposedly

---

1   See, for example, Luce Irigaray, *This Sex which Is Not One,* trans., Catherine Porter with Carolyn Burke (Ithaca, NY: Cornell University Press, 1985).

2   Sharon Olds, *Odes* (London: Jonathan Cape, 2016).

3   Kate Kellaway, "*Odes* by Sharon Olds Review—In Praise of Tampons and Other Taboos," *The Guardian,* 11 October 2016.

uncontrollable sexual impulses of women (the presumption always being that such impulses were appropriate subjects for derision rather than celebration).

The implied dialogue with unnamed male poets contained in "To the vagina" and "To jealous wives" becomes explicit in the next group of poems addressed to Gwerful's peers, Llywelyn ap Gutun, Ieuan Dyfi, and Dafydd Llwyd. The exchanges with Dafydd and Llywelyn are spirited, humorous, and often challenging, as if Gwerful is provoking her addressee deliberately in order to elicit another poem in response. The poems, especially those to Dafydd Llwyd, suggest a close relationship expressed through lively poetic dialogue. Particularly in those poems asking Dafydd Llwyd questions about the future, there is a sense of an apprentice bard consulting her teacher. Elsewhere, though, the relationship seems closer to that between separated lovers, and there is also a comedic exchange of erotic squibs, suggesting that the relationship with Dafydd was more than platonic. The poem addressed to Ieuan Dyfi is somewhat different, in that it bears witness again to Gwerful's strong feminist allegiance. Her riposte to Ieuan Dyfi's embittered attack on his former lover, Red Annie, prompts from Gwerful an impressive tour-de-force of learned defence, in which she lists a series of *exempla* of virtuous women taken from a range of sources, Classical, biblical, and historical. Such lists in the tradition of the "querelles des femmes" can become tedious, or simply mechanistic, but Gwerful succeeds in sustaining the reader's interest through the sheer *brio* of her writing and the skill of her metrics. Given that Gwerful is eager to defend other women, it is tempting to speculate that she may have corresponded with other female poets in the same way that she does with the male poets included here. It is certainly the case that other medieval women writers, such as the aforementioned Christine de Pizan, had networks of female correspondents, and of course this tradition of female coteries persisted into the early modern period and to the eighteenth-century Bluestockings.[1] Unfortunately, no dialogic poems by Gwerful addressed to other women have yet been discovered, though Gwerful's example certainly inspired later Welsh women poets, as evidenced by the work of her namesake, Gwerful ferch Gutun, an example of which is included below (no. 24).

---

1   Such coteries also existed in Welsh contexts, as Sarah Prescott ably demonstrates in her essay "Archipelagic Coterie Space: Katherine Philips and Welsh Women's Writing," *Tulsa Studies in Women's Literature*, vol. 33, no. 2 (Fall, 2014) pp. 51–76.

Also included below are several *englynion* which are not dialogic in character, some of which are definitely by Gwerful and others very probably by her. These brief, four-line verses are among her best work, displaying her technical virtuosity and the vividness of her imagery. "To her husband for beating her" is another of her poems with contemporary relevance, giving a voice to the victim of domestic violence, and an angry, vindictive voice at that. Other *englynion* seem mere exercises in poetic ingenuity, such as the scatological "To her maid as she shits," while others, such as "A lad beside the bush," continue the theme of uncontainable female desire. "Wetting my petticoat" offers a glimpse of a woman for whom poetic expression is almost second nature—it gives the impression of having been dashed off by the frustrated poet just as she arrives home, soaked to the skin. The two *englynion* of slightly more dubious authorship; "The snow" and "The grave" are amongst the most beautiful individual works in this collection, one giving a lyrical picture of a snow-covered landscape and the other a sobering reminder of that lonely final resting place.

Future scholarship, one hopes, may uncover more works by Gwerful Mechain and other medieval Welsh women poets. It is also possible that more evidence will emerge to solve the puzzle of doubtful authorship. For the moment, though, it is a matter to celebrate, as Gwerful herself might have celebrated, the fact that we have this small body of work by a fifteenth-century woman poet who has a voice at once traditional and eccentric, a voice capable of serious devotion and riotous indecency.

# A Note on the Texts and Translations

Though earlier Welsh texts edited by Leslie Harries and others have been consulted in the preparation of this work, the present editor is, like every other twenty-first century scholar or translator working on Gwerful, particularly indebted to Nerys Ann Howells' now-standard edition, *Gwaith Gwerful Mechain ac Eraill* (Aberystwyth: Canolfan Uwchefrydiau Cymreig a Cheltaidd, 2001)—for her work on the texts themselves, but also for her many insights. For a full list of manuscript sources, see Howells' edition, and also Cathryn Charnell-White, ed., *Beirdd Ceridwen: Blodeugerdd Barddas o Ganu Menywod hyd tua 1800* (Llandybïe: Barddas, 2005). For details of the manuscripts of Dafydd ap Gwilym, see www.dafyddapgwilym.net.

The medieval Welsh texts present translators with some formidable challenges. In what follows, each original Welsh poem is accompanied by a facing-page literal translation into English; the facing page presentation is intended to facilitate close study by those with little or no knowledge of Welsh. Below the original poem on each page is a freer translation in rhyming couplets. The free translations aim to convey much of the tone and verve of the original, while also giving some sense of the complexities of the formal qualities of the Welsh original—the rhyme and, to a lesser extent, the metre.

The poems included in the "In Context" section at the end of the volume are accorded the same treatment as those by Gwerful—original text in Welsh with a literal translation on the facing page, and a a freer translation in rhymed patterns similar to those of the Welsh originals appearing directly below the original texts.

# POEMS BY

# GWERFUL MECHAIN

(A rhymed, free translation appears
directly below the original medieval Welsh,
with a literal translation and
explanatory notes on the facing page.)

## 1. Dioddefaint Crist

Goreudduw gwiw a rodded
Ar bren croes i brynu Cred,
I weled, weithred nid gau,
O luoedd Ei welïau,
Gwaed ar dâl gwedi'r dolur,
A gwaed o'r corff gwedi'r cur.
Drud oedd Ei galon drwydoll
A gïau Duw i gyd oll.
Oer oedd i Fair, arwydd fu,
Wrth aros Ei ferthyru,

❂ ❂ ❂

## 1. Christ's Passion

Christ immaculate on a wooden cross
Was placed, to redeem the world's loss.
Look at the legion of his lacerations
The dear blood after the humiliations
His body's blood after the passion!
The price his pierced heart paid was high,
God's flesh itself was cut and men stood by,
There was a sign and Mary stood to witness
The martyrdom of her son, who was blameless:

# 1. Christ's Passion[1]

A worthy great God was placed
On a wooden cross to redeem Christendom,[2]
To see, not a false act,
From the host of his wounds
Blood paid after the pain
And blood from the body after the blow.
Dear was His heart pierced through
And all of God's sinews.
It was cold for Mary,[3] who was a sign,
As she waited for His martyrdom,

---

1   *Dioddefaint Crist / Christ's Passion*   In the medieval manuscript texts of this and other
    poems by Gwerful, the author's name is often cited. Such citations are omitted in the texts
    provided here—though information about them is provided in the notes.

    There are sixty-eight extant manuscript copies of this cywydd, each with some varia-
    tions. The manuscripts are held in the University of Bangor, the British Library, Cardiff
    Central Library, and the National Library of Wales. The principal manuscript collections
    which include it are the Brogyntyn, Cwrt Mawr, Esgair, Mostyn, Llanstephan, and Peniarth
    collections.

    *Christ's Passion*   Poems narrating the story of Christ's passion were numerous in the
    middle ages in most European vernacular languages, including Welsh and English. Gwerful
    Mechain's *cywydd* tells the familiar story, focusing on the intensity of Christ's suffering on
    the cross, perhaps in order to make the story more immediate and affecting for the reader
    or listener. Enid Roberts has suggested that the poem may have been inspired by the image
    of the crucified Christ in a stained-glass window of Llanwrin church. See: Enid Roberts,
    *Dafydd Llwyd o Fathafarn*, Annual Literary Lecture of the National Eisteddfod, Maldwyn
    (1981) pp. 22–23. Nerys Ann Howells believes that the impressive church in Oswestry may
    have been a more likely inspiration for the poet. See: Nerys Ann Howells, *Gwaith Gwerful
    Mechain ac Eraill* (Aberystwyth: Canolfan Uwchefrydiau Cymreig a Cheltaidd Prifysgol
    Cymru, 2001) p. 127. On the other hand, the story was so familiar in the religious culture
    of the period and had been versified by so many other poets (including Dafydd ap Gwilym),
    that Gwerful Mechain may not have been evoking a specific place or image. Since no fewer
    than sixty-eight manuscript copies of this *cywydd* survive, we may assume that it was very
    popular for a considerable period of time. Though it does not have a noticeably female
    voice, it does display the poet's metrical skill and the ability of the *cywydd* form to express
    ideas and images in a succinct and memorable way.

2   *Christendom*   Christendom (*Cred*)—the noun "cred" means faith or belief but with a capi-
    tal letter indicates the Christian world or Christendom.

3   *Mary*   Mary—Christ's mother, the Virgin Mary. Gwerful does not focus particularly on
    Christ's mother, though devotional poems to the Virgin were common in the Welsh tradi-
    tion from the earliest times—see, for example, "Mab Mair," a poem dating perhaps from the
    tenth century and surviving in manuscript in the Red Book of Talgarth, 163b. See Marged
    Haycock, ed., *Blodeugerdd Barddas o Ganu Crefyddol Cynnar* (Aberystwyth: Barddas, 1994)
    pp. 113–20.

Yr hwn a fu'n rhoi'i einioes
I brynu Cred ar bren croes.
Gŵr â'i friw dan gwr Ei fron,
A'r un gŵr yw'r Oen gwirion.
Prynodd bob gradd o Adda
A'i fron yn don, frenin da.
Ni cheir fyth, oni cheir Fo,
Mab brenin mwy a'n pryno.
Anial oedd i un o'i lu
Fwrw dichell i'w fradychu:
Siwdas wenieithus hydwyll,
Fradwr Duw, a'i fryd ar dwyll,
Prisiwr fu, peris ar fwyd,
Ddolau praff, ddal y Proffwyd.
Duw Mercher wedi 'mwarchad
Ydd oedd ei bris a'i ddydd brad.
Trannoeth, heb fater uniawn,
Ei gablu'n dost gwbl nid iawn,

He it was who freely made the great sacrifice
On the Cross to free mankind from vice.
With a wound beneath his breast this man
(The same man is the tender Lamb)
Has bought every single Adam,
The good King, his breast a flood of blood.
Never again will we see one so good,
No King's son to buy us, until he comes again.
It was bitter that one of his own men
Should have betrayed him at the last,
It was the scheming flatterer Judas,
Deceiver of God, bent on dishonesty, the traitor
Took the pieces of silver and after supper,
With strong bonds, he snared the Prophet.
It was on Wednesday after he lay in wait
Cheap was His price on that ashen date.
Unjustly, the next day, he met his fate:
Brutally beaten upon the floor

He who gave his whole life
To redeem Christendom on a wooden cross.
A man with his wound under his breast,
And the same man is the tender Lamb.
He bought every degree of Adam,[1]
With his breast a wave, good king.
We will never have, unless He comes again,
A greater king's son to redeem us.
It was desolate that one of his own host
Used guile to betray him
Deceitful, flattering Judas,[2]
God's betrayer, intent on treachery,
He put a price on him, stayed after food,
Strong ropes to catch the Prophet.
On Wednesday after waiting
That was his price and the day of his betrayal
The next day, with no just cause,
He was sorely reviled wholly unjustly,

---

1  *Adam*  Adam—the first man, according to Genesis, but here, as in English, a synonym for "man" or "human being."
2  *Judas*  Judas Iscariot—the disciple who first betrayed Jesus Christ for thirty pieces of silver, narrated in the Gospels. See, for example, Mark 14.10–11.

A dir furn cyn daear fedd
A'i 'sgyrsio ymysg gorsedd
Oni gad, enwog ydiw,
Glaw gwaed o'r gwelïau gwiw.
Duw Gwener cyn digoni
Rhoed ar y Groes, rhydaer gri,
A choron fawr, chwerw iawn fu,
A roesant ar yr Iesu,
A'r glaif drud i'w glwyfo draw
O law'r dall i'w lwyr dwyllaw.
Trwm iawn o'r tir yn myned
Oedd lu Crist wrth ddileu Cred
A llawen feilch, fellÿn fu,
Lu Sisar pan las Iesu.
Wrth hud a chyfraith oediog
Y bwrien' Grist mewn barn grog
Er gweled ar Ei galon
Gweli fraisg dan gil Ei fron.

Sorely betrayed to the grave's door,
And scourged alike by rich and poor
Until there was, as is well known,
A rain of blood from the worthy wounds.
On Friday before they had their fill
They put him on the Cross, a cry rang shrill,
And they placed a bitter crown
On Jesus' head as he gazed down,
And as he did so Longinus the blind was healed
By the blood which dropped and his eyes unsealed.
With heavy hearts Christ's disciples left
That cursed place as they nursed their grief
But Caesar's mob were merry and elated,
Proud that they'd killed the man they hated.
Old laws and ignorance of good
Meant they nailed Christ to the rood,
And they saw beneath his heart
A huge wound cleaving his breast apart.

And dreadful injury before the earth of a grave
And was scourged amid the assembly
Until there was, it is well known,
A rain of blood from the worthy wounds.
On Friday before they had their fill,
He was placed on the Cross, a piercing scream,
And a great crown, it was very bitter,
They placed on Jesus,
And the cruel lance to wound him there
From the blind man's hand to deceive him thoroughly.
Very heavily from that place
Went Christ's host as Christendom was destroyed
And proud and joyful, just so,
Was Caesar's[1] host when Jesus was killed.
By deceit and ancient law
They sentenced Christ to hang
Though they saw on His heart
A broad gash under His narrow breast.

---

1   *Caesar*   Augustus Caesar, the first Roman Emperor (63 BCE–14 CE).

Ni bu yn rhwym neb yn rhi,
Ni bu aelod heb weli.
Marw a wnaeth y mawr wiw nêr
Yn ôl hyn yn ael hanner.
Ar ôl blin yr haul blaned
A dduoedd, crynodd dir Cred.
Pan dynnwyd, penyd einioes,
Y gŵr grym o gyrrau'r groes,
Sioseb a erchis Iesu
I'w roi'n ei fedd, a'i ran fu.
Pan godes, poen gyhydedd,
Cwrs da i'r byd, Crist o'r bedd,
Yna'r aeth, helaeth helynt,
Lloer a'r haul o'u lliw ar hynt,
A phan ddug wedi'r ffin ddwys
Ei bridwerth i baradwys,
Troi a wnaeth Duw Tri yn ôl
I'r ffurf y bu'n gorfforol.

Never was such a king so abused,
No-one there failed to see, yet no-one accused.
And then the lord God died
In the middle of the day, the turning of the tide.
After this torment the great sun took
A hue of darkness, and Christendom shook.
From the Cross they took down his body dear
And there approached Joseph of Arimathea,
Who laid Christ's body in his own grave,
And that was his role, that's what he gave.
When Christ rose up from the tomb,
After so much pain, to save us from our doom,
Then suddenly both sun and moon
Were dark both at midnight and noon,
And when he crossed like everyone who dies,
Paying the price to enter Paradise,
The God of the Trinity turned back once more
Returning to human form, the mortal shore.

No king was ever tied up so
No limb could not be seen.
The great worthy lord died
After this just before midday.
After the affliction the sun planet
Grew dark, Christendom trembled.
When they pulled down, lifetime's penance,
The man of power from the edges of the cross
Joseph[1] claimed Jesus
To put him in his own grave, and that was his part.
When he rose, equal pain,
A good course for the world, Christ from the grave,
Then there went, great trouble,
Moon and sun from their colours and paths,
And when beyond the sad bourne he paid
His ransom to paradise,
The God of the Trinity turned back
To the bodily form he had been.

---

1 *Joseph* Joseph of Arimathea was a rich man and secret follower of Jesus who, according to
the Gospels, was responsible for taking Christ from the Cross and burying him in his own
tomb. *See* John 19.38–40.

Duw Naf i'r diau nefoedd
Difiau'r aeth, diofer oedd,
Yn gun hael, yn gynheiliad,
Yn enw Duw, yn un â'i Dad.
Un Duw cadarn y'th farnaf,
Tri pherson cyfion y caf.
Cawn drugaredd a'th weddi,
Down i'th ras Duw Un a Thri.
Cael ennill fo'n calennig
Pardwn Duw rhag Purdan dig:
Profiad llawen yw gennym
Praffed gras y Proffwyd grym.

☸ ☸ ☸

The Lord God whose Heaven is certain,
He was wholly good, and endured great pain,
Oh generous sublime, our mainstay,
At one with your Father, be with us this day.
Though I see but one great Lord,
He is Three Persons in accord.
Grant our prayer that we have your mercy,
Grant that we gain the grace of the Trinity.
Let our New Year gift be to win
God's pardon from the Purgatory of sin;
Our most pure and precious asset
To gain grace from the powerful Prophet.

Lord God to the true heavens
Thursday he went, he was worthy,
Generous lord, mainstay,
In God's name, united with his Father.
One strong God I judge you,
Three just persons I have.
We will have mercy with your prayer
We will gain your grace God of the Three in One.
To win as a New Year's gift
God's pardon from woeful Purgatory:
A joyful experience it is we have
The best grace from the Prophet of power.

## 2. Angau a barn[1]

Pwy'n gadarn ddyddfarn a ddaw
A phob dyn a phawb danaw?
Y Gŵr a wnaeth gaerau ne'
O fewn dydd a fu'n diodde',
Hwn sai' byth a'i henw sy bur,
Alffa Omega eglur.
Pob brenin, pob rhyw wyneb,
Uchel yw'n wir uwchlaw neb,
Pob swyddwr, pawb sy heddiw,
Pall i'n dydd, pwy well no Duw?
Y Fo a wnaeth y fan eitha'
O flaen neb Ei fawl a wna'.
Dyfnder ac uchder i gyd,

❁ ❁ ❁

## 2. Death and Judgement

Who will be strong on the Day of Judgement
That's on its way, for man's abasement?
The Man who made the entire world
In just one day, He who suffered,
He will stand strong forever; He of the pietà,
He is the clear Alpha and Omega.
Every last king, every last beggar,
He is set truly high, without error,
While every one of us working today,
Will cease one day; turn to great God and pray.
He it was who made the greatest sacrifice
Give Him praise then for paying that price.
He is high and low, far and wide,

---

1 *Angau a barn*  This poem has survived in only one manuscript, namely Bangor (Penrhos) 1573, 240.

# 2. Death and Judgement[1]

Who will be strong on the Day of Judgement that's coming
To every man and everbody beneath him?
The Man who made the fortresses of heaven
In one day, he who suffered,
This one will stand forever and his name is pure,
A clear Alpha and Omega.[2]
Every king, every last face,
He is truly high above everyone,
Every server, everyone who exists today,
Will cease one day; who is greater than God?
He it was who made the greatest sacrifice
Give Him praise before anyone.
All depth and height,

---

1   *Death and Judgement*   In this devotional poem, Gwerful Mechain turns to the topic of
    death and judgement, also a common concern for poets in Wales from the earliest times—
    see Section 3 in Marged Haycock, ed., *Blodeugerdd Barddas o Ganu Crefyddol Cynnar* (Ab-
    erystwyth: Barddas, 1994) pp. 141–240. This *cywydd* emphasizes the brevity of human life
    and the inevitability of death and judgement; everyone, therefore, from the lowest to the
    highest, needs to be prepared for death, to have atoned for their sins, and to be ready to give
    an account of themselves before Christ. Gwerful offers a series of *exempla* of great men who
    have all succumbed to death and judgement, the moral being that if they did not escape
    judgement, neither will we. Siôn Cent is frequently regarded as the most distinguished
    Welsh medieval poet to have addressed this topic. Gwerful's poem has survived in only
    one manuscript, indicating that it was by no means as popular as her "Dioddefaint Crist,"
    possibly because its didacticism conveys a message that most of us are reluctant to hear, or,
    as Gwerful herself puts it in the poem, "Ofnwn Ŵr ni fyn i neb/Dwyn enw ond yn wyneb."
    (We fear the Man that no-one dares to name/But, nameless, he will meet us all the same.)

2   *Alpha and Omega*   Alpha and Omega are the first and last letters of the Greek alphabet;
    the phrase "alpha and omega" indicates a comprehensive wholeness, all-knowing, all-en-
    compassing. It is also explicitly identified with Jesus Christ in the book of Revelation, for
    example, in Chapter 1, verse 8: "I am Alpha and Omega, the beginning and the ending,
    saith the Lord, which is, and which was, and which is to come, the Almighty."

Camp a sai', cwmpas hefyd.
Duw sy'n gadarn dysgedig,
Di-feth dro'm, Duw fyth a drig.
Heb ddiwedd yw'r mawredd mau,
Heb ddiochri, heb ddechrau.
Iawn o ras i bob nasiwn
O fewn ei oes ofni hwn.
Mae swyddwr i maes iddaw,
Oes dros lu, astrus ei law,
A hwn a gyrch hŷn ac iau,
Ail i'r ing elwir angau.
Pob awenydd, pob wyneb,
Y drych noeth nid eiriach neb,
Yn feibion gwychion y gwŷr,
Gwragedd, merched, goreugwyr.
Ymgweiriwn, ymdrysiwn draw,
Mae'n gelyn yma i'n gwyliaw.
Bwrw a fyn bâr o'i fynwes

His compass exceeds us, his creation abides.
Omniscient God is steady, unmoving,
He never dies; he looks to us, unfailing.
With no end and no beginning,
Impartial is the great God's hand,
Imparting grace to every land
Fear him your whole life; obey his command.
He has a skillful servant who goes about his business
Throughout the ages, a man of stillness, swiftness,
And this one greets both young and old,
Leading them to death, anguished and cold.
Every poet, every lovely face, will one day
Brave the gaze of judgement without delay;
No-one will be saved, not stalwart sons, strong men,
Fair daughters, girls, the best of women.
So let us repent, let's prepare for that place,
Since the enemy, Death, here stares us in the face.
An arrow will fly from his bow of brass

His achievement stands, and also his compass.
God is steady and all-knowing,
He turns to us without fail; God lives forever.
Without end is the greatness of God,
Without bias, without beginning.
Just of grace to every nation
Within his life fear this one.
There is a servant who goes out for him,
An age over a host, his hand dexterous,
And this one greets old and young,
Second to the anguish called death.
Every poet, every face,
The naked look will save nobody,
Men who are brave sons,
Women, girls, best of men.
Let us prepare, let us mend ourselves for that place,
The enemy's here to watch us.
He wishes to fire an arrow from his breast

I bob rhai o'r bwa pres.
Ni rybudd y dydd a daw,
Ni yrr gennad ar giniaw.
Dug Adda, Duw a'i gwyddiad,
Yn ŵr byw a Noe o'r bad,
Dug Abram ddinam o'i ddydd,
Dug Foesen deg o'i feysydd,
A dug Ddafydd deg ddifai
Broffwyd a'i wŷr braff o'i dai.
Dug Iesu deg a'i weision
Oddi ar hyd y ddaear hon.
Myn hwn ar hynt, mae'n hwyrhau,
Duw'n annog, ein dwyn ninnau.
Ofnwn Ŵr ni fyn i neb
Dwyn enw ond yn wyneb.
A wnêl drwg heb ei ddiŵgiaw
Yn ddraig o dân i ddrwg daw;
Os daioni fo 'stynnir,

To strike each man's breast, letting no-one pass.
No warning there'll be of the day to come,
No dinner gong will sound, calling us home.
Every man who has lived has been taken by God:
Look, he took alive the fallen Adam,
But took also blameless Abraham,
Noah in his ark did not escape his rod,
While fair Moses was taken from his field;
The great prophet David to him did yield,
He and his strong men, who were no shield.
He took the disciples and immaculate Jesus
Away from this world; just so will he seize us.
Take note of these words, for it's getting late,
God will steal us away to meet our fate.
We fear the Man that no-one dares to name
But, nameless, he will meet us all the same.
As a fiery dragon he will come to the wicked
That do evil and have sins committed,

At everyone from his brass bow.
There will be no warning of the day to come,
He will not send a messenger for dinner.
He took Adam, God knows,
A live man and Noah[1] from the ark,
He took spotless Abraham[2] from his day,
He took fair Moses[3] from his fields,
And he took fair blameless David[4]
The prophet and his strong men from their houses.
He took fair Jesus and his servants
From this wide world.
Realize this urgently, it's getting late,
God urges us, to steal us away.
We fear the Man that no-one wants
To name except when face-to-face.
He will come as a fiery dragon to evil ones
That do evil without repenting,
But the one who offers goodness,

---

1   *Noah*   Noah was the just man in the Old Testament who built an ark according to God's instructions in order to save the righteous and the animals from the great Flood sent by God to punish transgressive human beings. The story is told in Genesis, chapters 6–9.

2   *Abraham*   Abraham is the Old Testament patriarch who is made "the father of many nations" by God; see Genesis 17.

3   *Moses*   Moses was the Old Testament prophet and deliverer of the Hebrew people out of slavery in Egypt. He received the Ten Commandments from God on Mount Sinai. See Exodus 1–19.

4   *David*   David was an Old Testament King and poet, author of the Book of Psalms and, according to the Gospels, an ancestor of Jesus Christ. See Luke 3.31.

Ef a sai' hap i oes hir.
Duw a'n gwnaeth yn berffaith byd,
A Duw cyfion a'n dwg hefyd,
A Duw, wyneb daioni,
I wlad ne' eled â ni.

✿ ✿ ✿

But to those who do good and are strong,
The most he offers is that they will live long.
God made us a world immaculate,
And He, all righteous, will take us away from it
Benevolent God, when we are forgiven,
Will take us with him to the land of heaven.

He stands to have perhaps a long life.
God made us a perfect world,
And righteous God will take us away from it too,
And God, the face of goodness,
Will take us to the land of heaven.

## 3. Cywydd y cedor[1]

Pob rhyw brydydd, dydd dioed,
Mul frwysg, wladaidd rwysg erioed,
Noethi moliant, nis gwarantwyf,
Anfeidrol reiol, yr wyf
Am gerdd merched y gwledydd
A wnaethant heb ffyniant ffydd
Yn anghwbl iawn, ddawn ddiwad,
Ar hyd y dydd, rho Duw Dad.
Moli gwallt, cwnsallt ceinserch,
A phob cyfryw fyw o ferch,
Ac obry moli heb wg
Yr aeliau uwch yr olwg.
Moli hefyd, hyfryd tew,
Foelder dwyfron feddaldew,

✪ ✪ ✪

## 3. Poem to the vagina

Every poet, drunken fool,
Thinks he's just the king of cool,
(Every one is such a boor,
He makes me sick, I'm so demure),
He always declaims fruitless praise
Of all the girls in his male gaze,
He's at it all day long, by God,
Ignoring the best bit, silly sod:
He praises the hair, gown of fine love,
And all the girl's bits up above,
Even lower down he praises merrily,
The eyes which glance so sexily;
Daring more, he lauds the lovely shape
Of the soft breasts which leave him all agape,

---

1   *Cywydd y cedor*   There are 13 manuscript copies of this *cywydd*, located in the University of
    Bangor, the British Library, Cardiff Central Library, and the National Library of Wales.

# 3. Poem to the vagina[1]

Every drunken fool of a poet is quick
In his pompous vanity
(It is I who warrant it,
I of noble stock)
To sing of the girls of the lands
In fruitless praise all day long
But quite incompletely, by God the Father.
They praise a girl's hair, the mantle of fine love,
And every type of girl that's living,
And underneath they praise without complaining
The eyebrows above the eyes.
They also praise, beautiful plumpness,
The bare breasts, soft and smooth,

---

1 *Poem to the vagina* This is undoubtedly Gwerful's most notorious poem and, to judge by the many copies of it in the manuscript sources, one of her most popular. Some of the sources give it the even more explicit title of "Cywydd y gont" ("Poem of the cunt"). It appears to be a satirical poem written as a challenge to her male peers. It is possible that it is a counterpart and riposte to Dafydd ap Gwilym's "Cywydd y Gal" ("Poem to the Penis"; no. 25 below), although other poets of the time also wrote humorous verse about the male genitals (e.g. the anonymous *englyn* below and other works by poets such as Guto'r Glyn and Dafydd ab Edmwnd. See Dafydd Johnston, ed., *Canu maswedd yr oesoedd canol: Medieval Welsh erotic poetry* Cardiff: Tafol, 1991). Certainly Gwerful is using similar techniques to those of her male contemporaries, particularly in her use of '*dyfalu*,' in piling up the imaginative descriptions of a woman's genitalia. She is also taking to task the practices of her male peers as love poets, for, in praising the female beloved they praise all body parts except, the voice of the poem alleges, the most important.

The boldness and explicitness of Gwerful's erotic poem does not appear to have shocked her contemporaries, but it ensured that her work was neglected and concealed for many years by embarrassed male scholars after Wales became "a nation of Nonconformists" in the nineteenth century. (See the Introduction for further discussion of this point.)

A moli gwen, len loywlun,
Dylai barch, a dwylaw bun.
Yno, o brif ddewiniaeth,
Cyn y nos canu a wnaeth,
Duw yn ei rodd a'i oddef,
Diffrwyth wawd o'i dafawd ef.
Gado'r canol heb foliant
A'r plas lle'r enillir plant,
A'r cedor clyd, hyder claer,
Tynerdeg, cylch twn eurdaer,
Lle carwn i, cywrain iach,
Y cedor dan y cadach.
Corff wyd diball ei allu,
Cwrt difreg o'r bloneg blu.
Llyma 'nghred, teg y cedawr,
Cylch gweflau ymylau mawr,
Cont yno wrth din finffloch,
Dabl y gerdd â'i dwbl o goch,

And the beauty's arms, bright drape,
Even her perfect hands do not escape.
Then with his finest magic,
Before night falls, (it's tragic),
He pays homage to God's might,
An empty eulogy; it's not quite right:
For he's left the girl's middle unpraised,
That place where children are conceived,
The warm bright quim he does not sing,
That tender, plump, pulsating, broken ring,
That's the place I love, the place I bless,
The hidden quim beneath the dress.
You female body, you're strong and fair,
A faultless, fleshy court plumed with hair.
I proclaim that the quim is fine,
Circle of broad-edged lips divine,
A cunt there by a lavish arse,
Table of song with its double in red,

And praise the girl's arms like a bright curtain,
And both her hands; she deserves respect.
There, with his best magic,
He sang before nightfall,
His tongue giving fruitless praise
To God in his gifts and forgiveness.
But he leaves the middle without praise,
That palace where children are conceived,
The snug vagina, clear hope,
Tender and lovely, open circle strong and bright,
The place I love, delicate and healthy,
The quim beneath the cloth.
You are a body of boundless ability,
Pure court of feathery fat.
This is my credo, land of the quim,
A circle of lips with broad edges,
A cunt there by a lavish arse,
Table of song with its double in red,

Ac nid arbed, freisged frig,
Y gloywsaint wŷr eglwysig
Mewn cyfle iawn, ddawn ddifreg,
Myn Beuno, ei deimlo'n deg.
Am hyn o chwaen, gaen gerydd,
Y prydyddion sythion sydd,
Gadewch yn hael, gafael ged,
Gerddau cedor i gerdded.
Sawden awdl, sidan ydiw,
Sêm fach len ar gont wen wiw,
Lleiniau mewn man ymannerch,
Y llwyn sur, llawn yw o serch,
Fforest falch iawn, ddawn ddifreg,
Ffris ffraill, ffwrwr dwygaill deg,
Pant yw hwy no llwy yn llaw,
Clawdd i ddal cal ddwy ddwylaw.
Trwsglwyn merch, drud annerch dro,
Berth addwyn, Duw'n borth iddo.

And the churchmen all, the radiant saints,
When they get a chance, they've no restraint,
They never miss their chance to steal,
By St. Beuno, to give it a good feel.
So I hope you feel well and truly told off,
All you proud male poets, you dare not scoff,
Let songs to the quim grow and thrive,
Find their due reward and survive.
For it is silky soft, the sultan of an ode,
A little seam, a curtain, on a niche bestowed,
Neat flaps in a place of meeting,
The sour grove, circle of greeting,
Superb forest, faultless gift to squeeze,
Fur for a fine pair of balls, tender frieze,
Dingle deeper than hand or ladle,
Hedge to hold a penis as large as you're able,
A girl's thick glade, it is full of love,
Lovely bush, you are blessed by God above.

And the bright saintly men of the church
Don't abstain, highest blessing,
When they get a chance,
By St. Beuno,[1] to give it a good feel.
Because of this, a whip of rebuke,
To all you upright poets,
Be prolific in your songs to the vagina
Let them proliferate and gain reward.
It's silky, a sultan of an ode,
A little curtained seam on a lovely white cunt,
Flaps in a place of intercourse,
The sour grove, it's full of passion,
Great proud forest, faultless gift,
Fragile frieze, fur for a good pair of balls,
It's a hollow longer than a spoon or a hand,
A bush to hold a penis two hands wide;
A girl's thicket, precious ringlet of greeting,
Noble bush, may God save it.

---

1   *St. Beuno*   St. Beuno was a Welsh saint of the seventh century, particularly associated with
    North Wales. The poet Gerard Manley Hopkins studied in St. Beuno's Jesuit College near
    St. Asaph at the end of the nineteenth century, where he learnt Welsh and experimented
    with incorporating *cynghanedd* into English verse.

## 4. I wragedd eiddigus[1]

Bath ryw fodd, beth rhyfedda',
I ddyn, ni ennill fawr dda,
Rhyfedda' dim, rhyw fodd dig,
Annawn wŷd yn enwedig.
Bod gwragedd, rhyw agwedd rhus,
Rhwydd wg, yn rhy eiddigus?
Pa ryw natur, lafur lun,
Pur addysg, a'i pair uddun?
Meddai i mi Wenllïan,
Bu anllad gynt benllwyd gân,
Nid cariad, anllad curiaw,
Yr awr a dry ar aur draw.
Cariad gwragedd bonheddig

❀ ❀ ❀

## 4. To jealous wives

Jealousy is the strangest attitude:
It's no good thinking that everyone's lewd;
When you consider, it's really not nice,
You might even say it's a terrible vice,
But wives take on this inconvenient stance,
They're so suspicious, they look at me askance!
What is it in their nature, tell me please,
Makes them act so, never at their ease?
My friend Gwenllïan told me one time
That she'd heard sung a dirty old rhyme
That said it wasn't love on which women are sold,
That yearning which thrives on unreachable gold,
But what really gets wives going, bless their little cotton socks,

---

1   *I wragedd eiddigus*   This *cywydd* exists in only one manuscript, to be found in the National
Library of Wales 3050D (Mostyn 147), 360.

# 4. To jealous wives[1]

What sort of person, strangest of things,
Who won't get much good out of it,
Strangest of all, in some bitter way,
Especially unfortunate vice,
Why is it that wives, obstructive attitude,
Easily frowning, are too jealous?
What sort of nature, troubling image,
Makes them so, pure learning?
Gwenllïan[2] told me,
That at one time grey-haired song was indecent,
Not love, but lustful pining,
Now it turns towards gold yonder:
The love of respectable wives

---

1   *To jealous wives*   This cywydd is a humorous satire on women's sexuality, probably intended
    as a riposte to two varieties of verse by male poets that were common during the period—
    poems criticizing women for their supposedly uncontrollable sexual appetites, and poems
    about the stock figure of the jealous husband. The latter was characterized as a grumpy old
    man, often impotent, but fiercely possessive of his beautiful young wife. Gwerful's poem
    turns the tables on her male peers by alleging that it is women and not men who are insanely
    jealous and possessive of their husbands' sexual equipment, preventing any other desirous
    young woman from gaining access to it. The poem provides a good example of Gwerful's
    *dyfalu* in her description of the many things a jealous woman will sacrifice before she gives
    up her "cock." The latter is amusingly portrayed as an object almost independent of the
    husband himself, which the wife jealously guards, like a pampered pet. Although the poem
    does humorously attack jealous women, the overall effect achieved is a celebration of female
    sexuality, which is depicted as active and unbridled. Lustful men play very little part in the
    poem and that, perhaps, is its true satirical impulse—to turn the double sexual standards of
    the day on their head.
2   *Gwenllïan*   Dafydd Johnston suggests that Gwenllïan is a reference to another poet,
    daughter of Tudur Penllyn. See Dafydd Johnston, "Gwenllïan ferch Rhirid Flaidd," *Dwned*,
    III (1997) 29.

Ar galiau da, argoel dig.
Pe'm credid, edlid adlais,
Pob serchog caliog a'm cais,
Ni rydd un wraig rinweddawl,
Fursen, ei phiden a'i phawl.
O dilid gont ar dalwrn,
Nid âi un fodwedd o'r dwrn:
Nac yn rhad nis caniadai,
Nac yn serth er gwerth a gâi.
Yn ordain anniweirdeb
Ni wnâi'i ymwared â neb.
Tost yw na bydd, celfydd cain,
Rhyw gwilydd ar y rhiain
Bod yn fwy y biden fawr
Na'i dynion yn oed unawr,
Ac wyth o'i thylwyth a'i thad,
A'i thrysor hardd a'i thrwsiad,
A'i mam, nid wyf yn amau,

Is, pardon me for saying it, the love of good, big cocks.
Don't get het up, just believe me when I say
All these Mr Bigs are after me, desperate for a lay,
But these damn wives, so respectable,
Won't give up their cocks delectable,
Though they follow a girl in a field
Not an inch from their hand will they yield.
They're not having any, come what may,
Not for any price; not by night, not by day.
The jealous wife won't share the fun,
She won't do a deal with anyone.
Oh heck, it really is a pain,
This girl simply knows no shame:
What she likes best is a big cock and a good lay—
It means more to her than her family, any day,
Her own father and eight of her relations,
All her jewels and her fashionable creations,
Even her mother, I'm sad to say

For good cocks, a bad sign.
If you believe me, my angry voice,
Every well-hung would-be lover is after me,
But not one virtuous wife will give me,
The tease, her prick and her pole.
From following a cunt in a field,
It wouldn't go one inch from her fist:
Nor would she allow it freely
Nor if she were paid handsomely.
She would not condone adultery
By making a deal with anyone.
It's painful to think, delicate art,
That the girl is not ashamed
That the big cock means more to her
Even than her own family now,
More than eight of her relatives, and her father,
And her lovely treasure and its appearance
And her mother, I have no doubt,

A'i brodyr, glod eglur glau,
A'i chefndyr, ffyrf frodyr ffydd,
A'i cheraint a'i chwiorydd:
Byd caled yw bod celyn
Yn llwyr yn dwyn synnwyr dyn.
Peth anniddan fydd anair,
Pwnc o genfigen a'i pair.
Y mae i'm gwlad ryw adwyth
Ac eiddigedd, lawnedd lwyth,
Ym mhob marchnad, trefniad drwg,
Tros ei chal, trais a chilwg.
Er rhoi o wartheg y rhên
Drichwech a'r aradr ychen,
A rhoi er maint fai y rhaid,
Rhull ddyfyn, yr holl ddefaid,
Gwell fydd gan riain feinir,
Meddai rai, roi'r tai a'r tir,
A chynt ddull, rhoi ei chont dda

And her brothers, cousins, sisters, all away,
It's a tough old world when a common-or-garden dick
Strips a woman of her senses—it could really make you sick.
I know that libel is distinctly unsavoury,
But it's envy that causes it, don't you agree?
For there's a blight on this, my country,
And that heavy weight is jealousy,
In every marketplace it's just bad news,
Wrangling over a cock gives us the blues.
Some say a pretty girl would sooner
Than give up her very own peter,
Sacrifice eighteen of the landlord's cows
Or even the oxen that pull the ploughs,
Or an entire flock of sheep, so rash,
Or the estate, the buildings, and the cash,
Or even her own pussy, would you believe?

And her brothers, loud clear praise,
And her cousins, like brothers in the faith,
And her relations and her sisters:
It's a hard world when a penis
Leaves a woman bereft of her senses.
Slander is a wretched thing,
And it's jealousy that gives rise to it.
There's some plague on my land
And jealousy, heavy burden,
In every market, bad arrangement,
There is violence and suspicion over her cock.
Though one give eighteen
Of the lord's cattle and the plough oxen,
And all the sheep, rash summons,
And giving however much they're needed,
A lovely maiden would prefer,
Some say, to give away the houses and land,
And mind you, even her own good cunt,

Ochelyd, na rhoi'i chala,
Rhoi'i phadell o'i chell a'i chost
A'i thrybedd na'i noeth rybost,
Gwaisg ei ffull, rhoi gwisg ei phen
A'i bydoedd na rhoi'r biden.
Ni chenais 'y nychanon,
Gwir Dduw hynt, ddim o'r gerdd hon,
I neb o ffurfeidd-deb y ffydd
A fyn gala fwy no'i gilydd.

All the pans in her kitchen, you can't conceive,
The trivet they stand on, but not her naked post.
Rather her headdress and finery be forever lost
And her worldly goods, whatever the cost.
And let me tell you now at the end of my song,
This satire's not for her who wants a bigger-than-average dong.

Than give away her penis.
Rather give her frying pan from her pantry and its cost
And her trivet than her naked, sturdy post.
In her haste, she'd rather give her headdress
And all her possessions than her prick.
I did not sing my satire,
True to God, none of this poem,
For anyone of the shapeliness of the faith,
Who hankers after a bigger than usual cock.

## 5. I Lywelyn ap Gutun[1]

Dafydd o ymyl Dyfi,
Un glod â Nudd i'n gwlad ni,
Llywydd â gwayw onwydd gwyn,
Llew o aelwyd Llywelyn,
Tâl mewn grisial goreuserch
Lwys hardd o fetelau serch.
Haerwyd ym herwa o'i dir
Fal Gutun o foly goetir,
A chael ffyrdd, heb ochel ffo
Brawd Odrig yn bwrw didro
Ef a ddyfawd wiw Ddafydd
Llwyd ei ben (gwylltiaw y bydd),

❂ ❂ ❂

## 5. To Llywelyn ap Gutun

Dafydd from the banks of the Dyfi
As renowned as Nudd in our country,
Leader with a spear of white ash,
Lion from great Llywelyn's hearth,
Brave lover clear as crystal,
Bright jewel of love's mettle.
I was banished from his land
Like Gutun, who praised the woodlands,
And on my flight found the secret ways
Of Brother Odoric on his wanderings.
Worthy Dafydd will always say
Though his hair be grey (he'll be livid—very)

---

1    *I Lywelyn ap Gutun*    There are 8 manuscript copies of this poem, located in the University
of Bangor and the National Library of Wales.

# 5. To Llywelyn ap Gutun[1]

Dafydd[2] of the banks of the Dyfi[3]
As renowned as Nudd[4] in our country,
Leader with a spear of white ash
A lion of Llywelyn's[5] hearth,
A payment in crystal of the best love
A handsome jewel of the metals/weapons of love.
It was alleged that I was banished from his land
Like Gutun[6] who praised the woodlands
And found the paths, without avoiding flight,
Of Brother Odoric[7] on his wanderings.
Fine Dafydd, he will say
His hair is grey (he'll get mad)

---

1   *To Llywelyn ap Gutun*   This *cywydd* is one of a number by Gwerful Mechain where she is in a verse dialogue with another (male) poet or poets. Here, she refers mainly to her poetic sparring partner Dafydd Llwyd of Mathafarn, and to the eponymous Llywelyn ap Gutun (fl. 1480), another poet, who seems to have been an (ineffectual) go-between. Compare numbers 21 and 22 below. Dafydd Llwyd o Fathafarn (fl. 15th century) was a poet, contemporary, and probable lover of Gwerful Mechain. Apart from his poetic exchanges with Gwerful Mechain (see poems no. 7, 8, 9, 10, 17, 21, 23) he is best known as the author of prophetic verses, foretelling the coming of the "*Mab Darogan*" (the "Son of Prophecy," saviour of the Welsh people). It is likely from the evidence of the poems that Dafydd was considerably older than Gwerful. In this poem Gwerful sings the praises of Dafydd and heaps insults upon Llywelyn as a useless friend who is more interested in sheep and money than in helping the separated lovers. The tone is humorous and probably designed to prompt a poetic riposte from Llywelyn ap Gutun, as the final couplet suggests.
2   *Dafydd*   Dafydd Llwyd of Mathafarn (see above).
3   *Dyfi*   Dyfi, sometimes anglicized as Dovey, is a river which rises in the mountains above Dinas Mawddwy and flows to the sea at Aberdyfi. Dafydd Llwyd's house, Mathafarn (this mutates to "Fathafarn" after a preposition such as "o") was situated on the north bank of the Dyfi, near Llanwrin, in the old county of Montgomeryshire. There is still a house on the site but it dates from c. 1800.
4   *Nudd*   Nudd, along with Mordaf and Rhydderch, was one of the legendary Three Generous Men mentioned in the *Trioedd Ynys Prydain* (the Welsh Triads), medieval texts preserved in several manuscripts, including Peniarth 16.
5   *Llywelyn*   Nerys Howells indicates that this refers to the title character, Llywelyn ap Gutun (fl. 1480), poet and contemporary of Gwerful Mechain and Dafydd Llwyd who exchanged poems with them, but the line appears to suggest rather Dafydd Llwyd's own noble genealogy.
6   *Gutun*   Nerys Howells suggests that this might be a reference to the poet Guto'r Glyn (c. 1412–c. 1493).
7   *Odoric*   Odoric (c. 1286–1331) was an Italian Franciscan friar renowned for his wanderings, including a journey to China.

Na cheir rhwng Môn a Cheri,
Yng nghof dyn, 'y nghyfoed i.
Ni ffown heb ddig na phenyd,
Ni phery bun yn ffo'r byd.
Cywir fydd merch, crefydd maith,
Er tramwy o'r tir ymaith,
A'm bryd oedd, ond bwrw dyddie,
Ddyfod i gydfod ag e.
Nid aeth ymaith, doeth emyn,
Eto ni ddêl at ei ddyn.
Am y ddwywlad, mi ddaliwn
Y carai Sais y cwrs hwn.
Ar Ddafydd, wiwryw ddifai,
Ddoeth ei ben, ydd aeth y bai,
Gyrru gŵr, gair o'i guraw,
Llwytu drwg yn llatai draw.
Gwaeth fydd ei 'wyllys, nid gwell,
A gâi'i amarch a'i gymell.

That you won't find between Môn and Ceri
Such a girl as me, not in human memory.
But I had to flee, causing sorrow and pain,
A girl must escape in the dark, that's for certain.
Ultra-correct she must be, and pious,
As she passes through, or be thought devious.
All I wanted was to spend a day or two
To make a pact with him without more ado.
Anyway, the messenger failed to come
And he has yet to reach this woman.
He comes and goes according to his whim:
I'll bet an Englishman could do better than him.
And yet it was Dafydd who was at fault,
Wise, handsome, lovely and yet he called
This swarthy incompetent to take his message,
And now, mark my words, we have this wreckage.
His will turns out worse, not better,
When's he's urged on, to his dishonour.

That there's not to be found between Môn and Ceri[1]
In human memory, my equal.
I couldn't flee without causing pain and sorrow,
A girl can't be seen escaping from the world.
A woman must be correct, greatly religious,
In her passage out of the land
And my desire was just to spend a few days
To come to be with him.
He did not go away, wise hymn,
And he has yet to reach his (wo)man.
As for the two countries, I'd wager
That an Englishman would love this course.
It was handsome perfect Dafydd's fault
Despite his wisdom, for he sent,
Mark my words,
A bad grey man over as a messenger.
His fate will be worse, not better,
Whoever gets by force his dishonour.

---

1   *between Môn and Ceri*   Môn is the island of Anglesey off north-west Wales, while Ceri refers to a region near the English border in Powys in the south-east. The phrase was proverbial, and indicates a distance which spans the whole expanse of Wales, rather in the way that "from Lands' End to John O'Groats" is used in modern English discourse.

Ni wnâi, ni fynnai f'annerch,
Lywelyn ymofyn merch,
Nac iddo'i hun, bun a ball,
Na'i beri i neb arall.
Gynt yr oedd heb ganto'r un
Ac eto fal y Gutun,
Caru, ceisio crocyswr,
Defaid a gyriaid y gŵr,
Caru gwlân cyn cweiriaw gwledd
A chlydwr i'w foch lwydwedd,
A'r ŷd a wnâi iddo redeg
Drwy'r ddôr i'r Un Dre' ar Ddeg.
Ŷd o Swydd, ni edis un,
Ymhwythig oedd amheuthun.
Swydd yn nes sydd yn eisiau
A fynnai hwn i'w fwynhau:
Cynnar, lle gwelo cannyn,
Y try Duw naturiau dyn.

Llywelyn didn't greet me, nor show his face
To seek and ask for any woman in this place,
Either for himself (any girl would say no!),
Or on behalf of any other beau.
He went on his way without embracing one
And yet just like that other Gutun,
He loves nothing more than a legal brawl
And the man sure loves sheep, it's sheep above all,
For he's a drover, and wool comes first,
Wool comes before preparing a feast,
And he loves to shelter his grey-faced swine,
Scuttling over the border as far as Croesfaen
To get his corn, which means that there remains
In the whole of Shropshire not a single tasty grain.
The man needs a nearer county
To seek out and enjoy such bounty,
Where a hundred men see that grain ripens soon,
And where God turns human natures good.

He didn't want to greet me, nor did he,
Llywelyn, seek and ask for any woman,
Either for himself, (any girl would say no),
Nor on behalf of anyone else.
He was freer without embracing one
And yet just like Gutun,
He loved a legal wrangle
And the man loved sheep, he was a drover,
He loved wool before preparing a feast
And he sheltered his grey-faced pigs
And he ran to get his corn
Over the border to Croesfaen[1]
Not in Shropshire[2] remains
A single tasty grain.
He needs a nearer county
He'd like to enjoy that:
Where grain ripens early, as a hundred men can see
Where God turns human natures.

---

1    *Croesfaen*    Croesfaen was a town near Shrewsbury (see below).
2    *Shropshire*    Amwythig was, and still is, the Welsh name for Shrewsbury, a town in the English border county of Shropshire today. In earlier times it was Welsh territory, as indicated for example by the geography adumbrated in the *Canu Heledd* (c. 800–900).

Duwmawrth yn gwisgo damasg,
A choler wen uwchlaw'r wasg;
Trannoeth, meddai blant Ronwen,
Ŷd ar ei war o'r Dre-wen.
Drud fydd wrth ei drawiad fo
Drwy'r byd heb droi ar beidio,
A'i fryd oedd, afraid iddaw,
Fyned yr Ŵyl i Fôn draw.
A doeth draw, nid aeth drwodd,
Er yn rhaib, a'i arian rhodd.
Da oedd gael dyddiau gwylion
Gwin a medd ac wyna ym Môn;
Wyna, defeita eto,
Gwynedd fraisg, gyfannedd fro,
Alecsander a'i werin
Aeth ar draws i weithio'r drin,
I ymwybod rhag bod bâr
Mawr duedd môr a daear:

✿ ✿ ✿

Wearing damask he was on Shrove Tuesday,
The waistcoat and collar, the full array.
Next day, according to the children of Rhonwen,
On his back was a sack of grain from Dre-wen.
He strides out bravely with a swagger
Endlessly walking the world, the blagger,
And his purpose is, it's always the way,
To make it to Môn for the next feast day.
And when he comes over he gets paid too,
Though his booty is stolen, I tell you true.
Ah, it was good to have those days of feasting
Wine and mead in Môn—and lambing,
He's at it, sheep rustling, once again,
In the homeland, Gwynedd, the land of the grain.
The great Alexander and all his host
Travelled all over to conquer the most,
To make quite sure there was no place left free
He toured many regions of earth and sea:

On Shrove Tuesday wearing damask,
A white collar showing above his waistcoat,
The next day, say the children of Rhonwen,[1]
He had a sack of grain on his back from Dre-wen.[2]
He will stride out bravely
Through the world without a stop,
And his aim was always, it goes without saying,
To make it over to Môn for the feast day.
And he came over, he did not go through,
Though it was (stolen) booty, he got given his money.
It was good to have feast days
Wine and mead and delivering lambs in Môn;
Lambing, sheep rustling again,
In lush Gwynedd, the homeland.
Alexander[3] and his people
Went over to do battle,
To make sure there was no wrath
Many regions over earth and sea:

---

1  *Rhonwen*  Rhonwen (Rowena) was Hengist's daughter, who was married off to Gwrtheyrn, King of the Britons. "Rhonwen's children" therefore means the English (or Saxons).
2  *Dre-wen*  Whittington, in Shropshire.
3  *Alexander*  Alexander the Great (356–323 BCE) was a King of Macedon who came to rule, through successful military campaigns and conquest, over one of the most extensive empires of the ancient world.

Caru fal y concwerwr
Cerdded â gyried y gŵr.
O câi Wynedd Uwch Conwy
Ni ddwedai na mynnai mwy.
Minnau, ar ôl ymannerch,
Er ys mis a rois 'y merch.
Nis gwn, lle'r henwais gannyn,
P'le ydd a' rhag pla o ddyn.
Nid oes dre' er distrywio
Neu wlad fawr na weled fo.
Peidied, gwerthed y gorthir,
Gwastated ynn gwest y tir,
Oni rydd ym yn frau dda
Fwtieth am ei ddefeita.


❁ ❁ ❁


He made love like a conqueror,
And, like a drover, he was a wanderer.
If Gwynedd Uwch Conwy fell into his hands
He'd have no more to long for, no other lands.
For myself, since I last bid farewell to you,
It's been four weeks of loneliness, feeling blue.
Where the plaguey man was I hadn't a clue
Even though I asked a hundred or two.
Not a town stands that he hasn't razed,
Nor is there land on which he's not gazed.
So don't, for the sake of the uplands and plain,
Give this man a welcome, rather disdain,
Unless, that is, he gives me recompense
For all his sheep rustling nonsense.

He loved like the conqueror
It was walking that drove him on.
If he were to get hold of Gwynedd Uwch Conwy[1]
He would have no more to say or to desire.
For myself, since I last bid farewell to you,
It's been a month of loneliness for this woman.
I didn't know where the plague of a man was,
Though I named a hundred men.
There's no town he hasn't destroyed,
Nor land that he hasn't clapped his eyes on.
Don't, for the uplands' and plains' sake,
Give this man hospitality,
Unless he gives me generous
Compensation for all his sheep rustling.

---

1   *Gwynedd Uwch Conwy*   Gwynedd Uwch Conwy was the area of north Wales west of the
river Conwy (including the island of Anglesey).

# 6. I ateb Ieuan Dyfi am gywydd Anni Goch[1]

Gwae'r undyn heb gywreindeb,
Gwae'r un wen a garo neb;
Ni cheir gan hon ei charu
Yn dda, er ei bod yn ddu.
Lliw yr un nid gwell o rod
Y nos pan elo'n isod.
Gwen fonheddig a ddigia,
Naws dydd, oni bydd was da.
Nid felly yn gwna'r ddu ddoeth:
Ei drinio a wna drannoeth.
O dyfod Ieuan Dyfi
Rhai drwg yn amlwg i ni,
Rhai o'r gwynion fydd gwenwyn,

❁ ❁ ❁

# 6. A response to Ieuan Dyfi's poem on Red Annie

Woe betide you, incompetent bard,
Who sings the praise of the chaste blonde,
While the loving, clever dark one
Gets lambasted and shunned.
But a pretty girl's colour matters not a jot
Under cover of darkness, when passion's hot.
A well-bred white girl will sulk and mope
Unless you serve her like a dope,
But the wise dark girl will have her say:
She'll give you what for the very next day.
Oh Ieuan Dyfi, do come along,
When you say girls are bad, you're just plain wrong.
Though some of the fair ones really are poison

---

1   *I ateb Ieuan Dyfi am gywydd Anni Goch*   There are 5 manuscript copies of this *cywydd*, located in the British Library, Cardiff Central Library, and the National Library of Wales.

# 6. A response to Ieuan Dyfi's poem on Red Annie[1]

Woe to any person without skill,
Woe to a fair girl who loves no-one;
This one is not loved
Well, because she is dark.
Neither colour is necessarily better
When night falls.
The proud fair one will be offended,
By day, unless you are a good servant.
The wise dark one won't do that:
She will handle him the next day.
Oh say (then) Ieuan Dyfi[2]
Some of us are evidently bad,
Some of the fair ones are poisonous,

---

1  *A response to Ieuan Dyfi's poem on Red Annie*   This is another dialogic poem, written in response to that of Ieuan Dyfi, "I Anni Goch": see below, no. 20. It can be regarded as part of the European tradition of the "querelles des femmes," discussed by Ceridwen Lloyd-Morgan in her essay "The 'Querelle des Femmes': A Continuing Tradition in Welsh Women's Literature," in *Medieval Women: Texts and Contexts in Late Medieval Britain: Essays for Felicity Riddy*, ed. Jocelyn Wogan-Browne et al. (Turnhout: Brepols, 2000) pp. 101–14. Anni Goch is likely to have been a nickname; "coch" (red, which mutates to "goch") in Welsh may have been an indication of the colour of her hair. On the other hand, 'coch' may also indicate indecency or bawdiness in Welsh, in the same way that "blue" is used in English, so the epithet may be hinting at her character. In defending Annie Goch against Ieuan Dyfi's misogynistic rant, Gwerful speaks up for all women, providing *exempla* of virtuous women throughout the ages. The *cywydd* displays Gwerful's facility in using wide-ranging and erudite allusions to bolster the authority of her argument and voice. For further discussion of the poem, see Marged Haycock, "Merched drwg a merched da: Ieuan Dyfi v. Gwerful Mechain," in *Ysgrifau Beirniadol* XVI (1990) pp. 97–110.

2  *Ieuan Dyfi*   Ieuan Dyfi (fl. late fifteenth century) was a poet and contemporary of Gwerful Mechain, probably from Aberdyfi in Meirionethshire, who wrote in the *cywydd* form. He is the author of "To Red Annie" (poem 20 below), to which Gwerful's poem is a response.

A rhai da a urdda dyn.
Merch a helethe Eneas,
Ddu rudd, ac oedd dda o ras.
Gwenddolen a ddialodd
Ei bai am na wnaid ei bodd.
Gwraig Ddyfnwal yn gofalu
A wnâi les rhwng y ddau lu.
Marsia ffel, gwraig Guhelyn,
A ddaeth a'r gyfraith dda ynn;
A gwraig Werydd, ddedwydd dda,
Heddychodd, hyn oedd iacha',
Rhwng dau lu, mawr allu maeth,
Mor felys rhag marfolaeth.
Mam Suddas, oedd ddiraswr,
Cywir a gwych carai'i gŵr,

✿ ✿ ✿

While some of us dark ones have virtue and reason.
It was a woman who made Aeneas rich:
Dido was noble, and dark as pitch.
Gwenddolen was one who got her own back
When her will wasn't done; she just had the knack.
Tonwen, she who was Dyfnwal's wife,
As leader she kept the land free of strife.
Intelligent Marcia, Cuhelyn's consort,
Sorted our Laws and cleaned up the court.
Venissa, who was Gwerydd's wife,
She too brought peace and long life,
Standing between two raging battalions,
She brought sweetness not death to those rapscallions.
Tiborea, the mother of Judas the traitor,
She was a loving wife, don't hate her,

And some are good and honour a man.
(It was) a woman who magnified Aeneas,[1]
Dark-cheeked, she was graceful and good.
Gwendolen[2] took her revenge
For her wrong since her will was not done.
Dyfnwal's wife[3] made sure
That she did good between the two hosts.
Wise Marcia,[4] Cuhelyn's wife,
Brought us the good system of law;
And Gwerydd's wife,[5] content and good,
Made peace, which was the safest (thing to do),
Between two hosts, great ability and nurturing,
So sweet against death.
The mother of Judas,[6] who was a wicked man,
Was faithful and noble and loved her husband,

---

1  *Aeneas*  Aeneas was a Trojan prince who escaped after the fall of Troy and, after many
   wanderings, settled in Italy. He is seen both as the founding father of the Roman people (an
   ancestor of Romulus and Remus) and a progenitor of the Britons, through his grandson,
   Brutus. He is a relatively minor caracter in Homer's *Iliad* but of course takes centre stage in
   Virgil's *Aeneid* (29–19 BCE). It is there that his sojourn in Carthage is most fully narrated;
   while there he falls in love with Queen Dido but then abandons her when his mother,
   Venus, reminds him of his destiny. When she finds that she has been abandoned, Dido
   commits suicide. Although she is not named in Gwerful's poem, it is she who is seen as the
   noble figure in the relationship.
2  *Gwendolen*  Gwendolen was a Queen of Britain in the eleventh century BCE, according
   to Geoffrey of Monmouth. She was the daughter of Corineus, a Cornish ruler, and was
   married to King Locrinus of the Britons, the eldest son of Brutus. However, Gwendolen
   was spurned by her husband in favour of his mistress, Esyllt. Gwendolen raised an army in
   Cornwall, defeated and killed her former husband in battle, and went on to reign success-
   fully for fifteen years, before abdicating in favour of her son.
3  *Dyfnwal's wife*  Dyfnwal's wife was Tonwen, renowned for standing between two armies
   and preventing them from going into battle, thus saving many lives. Dyfnwal was a King of
   Cornwall and, later, a king of the Britons.
4  *Marcia*  Marcia was married to another legendary King of the Britons, Cuhelyn. She be-
   came Queen in her own right after the death of her husband, ruling until her son came of
   age. Geoffrey of Monmouth speaks highly of her intelligence and wisdom. She is credited
   with devising the *Lex Martiana*, a code of law which was later translated into English by
   Alfred the Great, forming the basis of Mercian Laws.
5  *Gwerydd's wife*  Gwerydd's wife was Genuissa, or Venissa, who was the daughter of the
   Roman Emperor Claudius. According to Geoffrey of Monmouth, she successfully mediated
   between the Britons and the Romans, preventing further warfare.
6  *mother of Judas*  The mother of Judas Iscariot was Cyborea or Tiborea. Mentioned in Apoc-
   ryphal sources, she is meant to have had a prophetic dream that she would give birth to a
   child who would bring about the destruction of the Jewish people but when she tried to
   warn people of this, she was ignored.

A gwraig Beiled, pei credid,
Y gwir a ddywad i gyd.
Elen merch Goel a welynt,
Gwraig Gonstans, a gafas gynt
Y Groes lle y lladdwyd Iesu,
A'r gras, ac nis llas mo'i llu.
Wrth Gwlan, fu un waneg,
A ddoeth yr un fil ar ddeg
O'r gweryddon i'r gradde
Am oedd a wnaeth, i Dduw Ne'.
Gwraig Edgar, bu ddihareb,
A wnaeth yr hyn ni wnaeth neb:
Cerddodd yr haearn tanllyd
Yn droednoeth, goesnoeth i gyd,
A'r tân ni wnaeth eniwed
I'w chroen, mor dda oedd ei chred.
Eleias a ddanfonasyd
At wraig dda i gael bara a byd.

And Pontius Pilate's wife as well
Was the soul of truthfulness, so they tell.
Ellen, the daughter of Coel,
And wife of Constance, got by toil
The Cross on which Christ Jesus died,
And its grace, and her legions cried.
In Cologne were thousands of virgins
Who drowned in the sea, enduring pains,
But they received their reward in Heaven.
Edgar's wife was proverbial among men
She did what no other soul
Dared: walked barefoot on hot coal,
And the fire did her no harm
Since her faith just kept her warm.
Elijah the prophet sent out a message
To break bread, the world's famine to assuage;

And Pilate's wife,[1] to her credit,
Told the whole truth.
Elen daughter of Coel[2] they saw,
Wife of Constance, once obtained
The Cross on which Jesus was killed,
And the grace, and her host was not killed.
In Cologne there was a surge,
That took the eleven thousand
Virgins[3] to the depths
For what was done, to God in Heaven.
Edgar's wife[4] was proverbial,
And did something that no-one else had done:
She walked on the flaming iron
Barefoot, her legs uncovered,
And the fire did no harm
To her skin, so strong was her belief.
Elijah[5] was sent
To a good wife to get bread.

---

1   *Pilate's wife*   Pilate's wife is unnamed in the Gospels but later sources name her as Claudia or Claudia Procula. In Matthew 27.19 she is described as having a prophetic dream and attempts, in vain, to prevent her husband, Pontius Pilate, the prefect of Rome in Judaea, from having Christ crucified.

2   *Elen daughter of Coel*   Elen may be a reference to Saint Elen (or Helen), wife of the Roman Emperor Macsen Wledig, and founder of many churches in Wales, or to Saint Helena, who discovered the True Cross and was the mother of the Emperor Constantine. Confusion between these figures was, according to Marged Haycock, common; both saintly Helens of course provide an excellent counter-example to Ieuan Dyfi's Helen of Troy.

3   *eleven thousand Virgins*   This is a reference to a legend about St. Ursula who led that number of followers from the city of Cologne across the sea to be wives for the men of Brittany. Unfortunately, their ship sank and they met their martyrdom.

4   *Edgar's wife*   A slightly problematic reference, since there is no record of the wife of King Edward of England, Aelfryth, walking on hot coals or manifesting saintliness in other ways. Nerys Howells suggests that it may be a reference to Emma, mother of Edward the Confessor, who did walk on hot coals in order to prove that she was innocent of the charge of adultery.

5   *Elijah*   The Prophet Elijah was fed by an unnamed widow, as narrated in I Kings 9–24. Despite her own destitution, she feeds the prophet and he later repays her by reviving her dead son.

Gwraig a wnaeth pan oedd gaetha'
Newyn ar lawer dyn da,
O'r ddinas daeth at gasddyn
Dig i ddywedyd i'r dyn;
Troesai ei boen tros y byd,
Disymwth y dôi symud.
Susanna yn sôn synnwyr,
Syn a gwael oedd sôn y gwŷr.
Mwy no rhai o'r rhianedd,
Gwell no gwŷr eu gallu a'u gwedd.
Brenhines, daeres dwyrain,
Sy' abl fodd, Sibli fain,
Yn gynta' 'rioed a ddoede
Y down oll gerbron Duw Ne';
Hithau a farn ar yr anwir
Am eu gwaith, arddoedyd gwir.
Dywed Ifan, 'rwy'n d'ofyn,
Yn gywir hardd, ai gwir hyn?

This good woman did as she was asked,
As many starved, she balked not at the task.
Meanwhile in the city a man in bad humour
Decided to give out a false rumour;
He spread pain throughout the world
But he suddenly had to eat his words.
Susanna was good and full of good sense;
The men's rumours of her were to give offence.
Girls are the mildest of creatures,
They're better than men, in skill and features.
Queen and heiress of the Orient
Was the Sibyl, most excellent,
She was the very first to say
That 'fore God there'd be a Judgement Day;
For her wisdom all revered her
She was named truth-teller of the future.
Tell me, Ifan, I'm asking you,
Tell me now, isn't all of this true?

The wife did this when the worst
Famine afflicted many a good man,
From the city she came to a hateful man,
Angry, to say to the man;
His pain turned across the world,
Suddenly movement came (back).
Susanna[1] spoke sensibly,
The men's accusations were senseless and vile.
More than a few girls,
Have abilities and manners better than men's.
Queen, strong woman of the East,
Sharp Sybil,[2] clever in her ways,
Was the first ever to say
The whole truth before God in Heaven;
It was she who passed judgement on the liars
For what they'd done, she told the truth.
Tell me Ifan, I'm asking you,
Truly and nicely, is this true?

---

1  *Susanna*  Susanna was a beautiful young married woman who was spied upon by two
   lecherous old judges. When she came out into her garden to bathe alone, they attempted to
   rape her; she resisted and they subsequently accused her of adultery with a young man. She
   was saved from being condemned to death by the young prophet Daniel, who proved her
   innocence. The story is narrated in *Susanna* 1.1–64. It is a subject that has proved irresist-
   ible for many visual artists, including Rembrandt, who portray the naked Susanna and the
   elderly voyeurs. Perhaps the most striking visual representation of the story is by the woman
   artist, Artemisia Gentileschi, who depicts Susanna's fear and vulnerability before the old
   men's lechery in her 1610 work, *Susanna and the Elders*.
2  *Sharp Sybil*  There were a number of Sybils in ancient Greek culture; they were women
   deemed to be oracles, whose cryptic utterances were held to prophesy the future. It is likely
   that Gwerful is referring to the *Sibylline Oracles*, a collection of oracular texts brought to-
   gether in the sixth century CE, which foretell days of judgement and final apocalypse.

Ni allodd merch, gordderchwr,
Diras ei gwaith, dreisio gŵr.
Dig aflan, o dôi gyfle,
Ymdynnu a wnâi, nid am ne'.
Gad yn wib, godinebwr,
Galw dyn hardd gledren hŵr.
Efô fu'n pechu bob pen,
Ac o'i galon pe gwelen'.
Dywed Ifan, ar dafawd,
Rhodiog ŵr, cyn rhydu gwawd,
Ai da i ferch golli'i pherchen,
A'i phrynt a'i helynt yn hen?
Yr un ffŵl a neidio wrth ffon
Neu neidio wrth lw anudon,
Aed ffeilsion ddynion yn ddig,
Duw a fyddo dy feddyg.

❁ ❁ ❁

And when all is said and done
No woman could rape a mother's son,
Whatever the traitor had gone and done.
So stop your libel, you adulterer,
You who call a lovely girl a whore,
You who sin from morn to night,
Even deep in your heart, if I could see aright.
Tell me, Ifan, do you think it's just
For a wife to be chucked when her husband's lust
Decides she's too old for him?
An old fool leaps a stick to keep in trim,
Or to the magistrate's call gives a leap and a hop,
For false men like you just get in a strop;
I can't mend your pretended pain:
Let God heal your precious bane.

No woman could, fornicator,
Ever rape a man, your doings are wicked.
Evil, jealous man, if the chance came,
You would be pulled down, not towards heaven.
Stop your attacks, adulterer,
Calling a lovely woman a whore.
You're the one who's been sinning at both ends,
And in your heart if we could see into it.
Tell me, Ifan, on your tongue,
Roving man, before your mockery rusts,
Is it good for a woman to lose her possessions,
When she gets old and her appearance and troubles show?
The same fool who jumps when he is whipped
Or jumps to the oaths of magistrates,
False men take offence,
Let God be your physician.

# 7. Gwerful Mechain yn holi Dafydd Llwyd[1]

*Gwerful Mechain*

Pa hyd o benyd beunydd—yn gwylio
    Yn gweled byd dilwydd,
    A pha amser, ddiofer Ddafydd,
    Y daw y byd ai na bydd?

*Dafydd Llwyd*

Pan fo yr ych mawr uchod—anturiwr
    Yn tirio'n rhith Ffrancod,
    Yn ddewr ei arfau, yn dda'i arfod,
    Yn wâr gynt, yn ŵr y god.

✾ ✾ ✾

# 7. Gwerful Mechain questions Dafydd Llwyd

*Gwerful Mechain*

How long must we do this daily penance—waiting,
    Watching a wretched world's substance,
    Dear Dafydd, tell me when independence
    Will come, and the world once again advance?

*Dafydd Llwyd*

When the great ox comes to land—an adventurer
    Arrayed in the guise of a Frenchman,
    Brave in arms, at the head of his war band,
    Courteous, wealthy, skilled in command.

---

1  *Gwerful Mechain yn holi Dafydd Llwyd* These *englynion* exist in 5 manuscript copies, located in the British Library and the National Library of Wales.

# 7. Gwerful Mechain questions Dafydd Llwyd[1]

*Gwerful Mechain*

How long a daily penance—watching
    Seeing a wretched world,
    And when, worthy Dafydd,
    Will the world come which is not like this?

*Dafydd Llwyd*

When the great ox[2] above will be—an adventurer
    Comes to land in the guise of a Frenchman,
    Brave in arms, skilled in battle,
    Courteous before, a man of the treasury.

---

1  *Gwerful Mechain questions Dafydd Llwyd*   Dafydd Llwyd was particularly famed for his va-
ticinatory or prophetic verse (*canu brud*), so it is not unexpected to find Gwerful Mechain
(in this sequence of *englynion*) questioning him about what he sees in the future. Dafydd's
answer to Gwerful's question is somewhat cryptic, and cloaked in the typical symbolic lan-
guage of the prophetic verse of the time. He seems, however, to be prophesying the coming
of a saviour figure (*y Mab Darogan*) and to foresee battle, destruction, and final victory.

2  *the great ox*   Nerys Ann Howells suggests that the ox is a reference to Jasper Tudor; see
*Gwaith Gwerful Mechain ac Eraill*, p. 161. Jasper Tudor (1431–95) was Earl of Pembroke
and the uncle of Henry Tudor (who would become King Henry VII when he took the
English crown at the Battle of Bosworth in 1485). The Tudors were an indisputably Welsh
family originally from Penmynydd in North Wales. There is some evidence that Henry Tu-
dor actually stayed with Dafydd Llwyd in Mathafarn on his way to the Battle of Bosworth,
and that Dafydd prophesied his victory there.

Rhwng y naw a'r deunaw y dôn'—pob gofal
    A gofid gan ladron,
   A dinistr a wna dynion
   Rhai sydd yn yr ynys hon.

Neidr fain a'r glain i Golunwy—y rhed
    Ac i'r rhyd ar Gonwy,
   Neidr a fernir 'rhyd 'Fyrnwy,
   Nodi'r glain gynt glan Gwy.

Yna y gwŷl Gwerful y gorfod—ar y bryniau,
    A'r brenin mewn trallod
   Ar y mynydd 'Nghyminod,
   A min cledd yn mynnu clod.

�֍ �֍ ✖

Between ninth and eighteenth the enemy vile—crafty,
    Cunning and full of guile,
   Will come to deal destruction the while
   And death to some who are on this isle.

The adder and treasure to Colunwy—will chase,
    Up the stream in Conwy,
   The snake will be judged along the Fyrnwy,
   The treasure will triumph on the banks of the Wye.

Then Gwerful will witness victory—on the hills,
    And the king in distress we'll see,
   On Cyminod mountain we'll be set free,
   And the sharp sword's praise we shall decree.

Between the ninth and eighteenth they'll come—every care
  And worry by thieves,
  And destruction men will wreak
  Some who are on this island.[1]

A slim snake and treasure[2] to Colunwy—will run
  To the stream in Conwy,
  A snake will be judged along the Fyrnwy,
  To note the former treasure on the banks of the Wye.

Then Gwerful will see the victory—on the hills,
  And the king in distress
  On the mountain of Cyminod,[3]
  And the sharp weapon demanding praise.

---

1  *Between the ninth ... this island*  The prophetic poetry of medieval Wales foretold a time
   when a saviour (the *Mab Darogan*—Son of Prophecy) would come to reclaim the crown of
   Britain for Wales. "This island" would then be united under a Welsh crown. A number of
   historians have suggested that Welsh support for the Tudors was strongly influenced by this
   tradition of prophetic verse. See, for example, Glanmor Williams, *Recovery, Reorientation,
   and Reformation: Wales c. 1415–1642* (Oxford: OUP, 1993) p. 155.
2  *slim snake and treasure*  The "snake" denotes the enemy and the "treasure" (or gem) the
   hero, Jasper Tudor. The *englyn* traces the course of their coming battles along four rivers,
   Clun, Conwy, Vyrnwy, and Wye.
3  *the mountain of Cyminod*  This is a place name that occurs in the prophetic verses; its actual
   location is uncertain.

## 8. Gwerful Mechain yn gofyn i Dafydd Llwyd[1]

Ateb i'm hwyneb o'm hiaith—fanwl
  Am a fynwy'n ddilediaith,
  Pa bryd y cair, er Mair mawr iaith,
  Drwy Rufain yr un afiaith?

Pan ddêl aer yn daer o'r dyn—o Ladin
  I ledio pob dyffryn,
  Deliwch pan losger Dulyn
  Fe ddaw tro i hon trwy hyn.

Pan aner lloer, poen anian—osodiad,
  Ar Sadwrn Pasg Bychan,
  Yr ail Iau yn ôl Iyfan,
  Yn y tir ynynnir tân.

✿ ✿ ✿

## 8. Gwerful Mechain asks Dafydd Llwyd

Tell me to my face in my language—in detail
  Why don't you retail your message,
  When will there come, blessed Mary's image,
  From Rome, the news that releases from bondage?

When an heir springs from a woman's womb—in Latin
  He'll lead us out of the gloom,
  When Dublin burns, our valleys will bloom,
  The One will come, and end our doom.

When the face of the moon is half hidden away—a voice,
  Rejoice, on Little Easter Sunday,
  Will speak, and soon after St. John's Day
  All over the land the bonfires' flames will play.

---

1  *Gwerful Mechain yn gofyn i Dafydd Llwyd*  These *englynion* have survived in one manuscript copy, namely the National Library of Wales 1553A, 473.

## 8. Gwerful Mechain asks Dafydd Llwyd[1]

Answer me to my face in my language—in detail
    For I want to know clearly
    When will there be, for great Mary's sake,
    Throughout Rome,[2] the same high spirits?

When an heir[3] comes eagerly from a woman—from Latin
    To lead every valley,
    You will deal when Dublin[4] burns
    This one's turn will come through this.

When the moon is half full, pain of nature—a decree,
    On Little Easter Sunday,[5]
    The second Thursday after St. John's Day[6]
    In the land fires will be kindled.

---

1   *Gwerful Mechain asks Dafydd Llwyd*   This sequence of *englynion* by Gwerful Mechain is, like the previous exchange with Dafydd Llwyd (no. 7), in the tradition of prophetic or vaticinatory poetry, and is also addressed to Dafydd.

2   *Rome*   The reference to Rome here appears to allude to a tradition deriving from Geoffrey of Monmouth that the last Welshman to wear the crown of Britain, Cadwaladr, is buried there. Before his death, an angel informed him that no Welshman would rule Britain again until Cadwaladr's bones were returned there from Rome.

3   *an heir*   The heir mentioned here is the *Mab Darogan* mentioned over and over in the prophetic verses, who will come to save Wales and restore her sovereignty.

4   *Dublin*   Perhaps an allusion to a variation of the *Mab Darogan* prophecy, which is the *Mab Gwyddelig* (Son of Ireland), according to which the saviour figure will come to Wales from Ireland.

5   *Little Easter Sunday*   First Sunday after Easter Sunday itself.

6   *St. John's Day*   This could be a reference either to the feast of John the Baptist (June 24th) or to that of the apostle John (December 27th).

Cyn y dêl rhyfel daw rhyfeddod—ar y môr,
     Mawr yw gwyrthiau'r Drindod,
A'r prif ar naw'n profi'r nod,
Gwae ynys y gwiddanod.

✿ ✿ ✿

War will come with many wonders—from the sea,
     As great as the Trinity's marvels,
     And the fell chieftain will give a sign like thunder,
     The woeful witches' island will be torn asunder.

Before war comes there will come wonders—on the sea,
    The Trinity's miracles are great,
    And the terrible chief will give a sign
    Woe be to the witches' island.

## 9. Ymddiddan rhwng Dafydd Llwyd a Gwerful Mechain[1]

*Dafydd Llwyd*

Dywaid ym, meinir, meinion—yw d'aeliau,
    Mae d'olwg yn dirion,
      Oes un llestr gan estron,
      A gwain hir y gannai hon?

*Gwerful Mechain*

Braisg yw dy gastr, bras gadarn—dyfiad
    Fal tafod cloch Badarn;
      Brusner cont, bras yn y carn,
      Brasach no membr isarn.

✿ ✿ ✿

## 9. Conversation between Dafydd Llwyd and Gwerful Mechain

*Dafydd Llwyd*

Tell me, lovely girl, whose brows are slender,
    Your expression is tender;
      Do you, strange girl, have a big enough receptacle,
      A sheath long enough to accommodate this tackle?

*Gwerful Mechain*

Bold is your dick, well-hung and hard,
    Like the bell of Saint Padarn's tongue
      Vagina's prisoner, proud at its snout,
      Like the shaft of a pole axe, so stout.

---

1  *Ymddiddan rhwng Dafydd Llwyd a Gwerful Mechain*  These *englynion* exist in 3 manuscript copies, one of which is to be found in the National Library of Wales (7191B), and two of which are in the Llanstephan collection (167, 34 and 173, 177).

# 9. Conversation between Dafydd Llwyd and Gwerful Mechain[1]

*Dafydd Llwyd*

Tell me, lovely girl, slender are your brows,
    Your look is tender;
    Does a stranger have any dish,
    And a long sheath which would contain this?

*Gwerful Mechain*

Sturdy is your cock, stout strong growth
    Like the clapper of Padarn's[2] bell;
    Prisoner of a cunt, stout at its hilt,
    It's stouter than a pole-axe's shaft.

---

1   *Conversation between Dafydd Llwyd and Gwerful Mechain*  A sharp contrast in tone to the previous prophetic verses, this exchange of *englynion* between the two poets is joyfully erotic. Dafydd wonders boastfully whether any woman has a vagina long enough to accommodate his member, and Gwerful gives him his answer. She acknowledges the large size of Dafydd's sexual equipment and goes on to celebrate the joys of sexual intercourse. Dafydd Johnston suspects that the question and answer are both by Dafydd Llwyd, but there is no doubt that Gwerful was perfectly capable of writing in this overtly indecent manner. Howells suggests that she may be taking on the stock persona of the "unruly woman." According to Dafydd Johnston, court records from the period show that a man would frequently display his penis as an enticement to a woman to make love, and some such situation is certainly indicated in this exchange of *englynion*. See: D.R. Johnston "The erotic poetry of the cywyddwyr," *Cambridge Medieval Celtic Studies*, 22 (Winter, 1991) 63–94.

2   *Padarn*  Padarn was a 6th century saint who founded a church in Llanbadarn near Aberystwyth. He is also associated with Brittany. The oldest bells of the current St. Padarn's church date from the mid eighteenth century, so it is impossible to tell whether the original bell of Saint Padarn had a longer than usual clapper, as the poem suggests. Dafydd ap Gwilym also compares the penis with a bell's clapper; see "Cywydd y Gal" below, no. 25, l. 34.

Hwde bydew blew, hyd baud blin—Ddafydd,
    I ddofi dy bidin;
    Hwde gadair i'th eirin,
    Hwde o doi hyd y din.

Haf atad, gariad geirwir—y macwy,
    Dirmycer ni welir.
    Dof yn d'ôl oni'm delir,
    Y gwas dewr hael â'r gastr hir.

Gorau, naw gorau, nog arian—gwynion
    Gynio bun ireiddlan;
    A gorau'n fyw gyrru'n fuan
    O'r taro, cyn twitsio'r tân.

❁ ❁ ❁

So, Dafydd, before you're pooped, here's a downy crater
    To tame your pecker;
    Here's a perch for your peaches,
    Here you go: get to the upper reaches.

I'll come to you if your love is true, bold lad,
    For I like what I can see of you;
    I'll follow you if I'm not held back,
    Brave, noble lad with the lengthy cock.

The best thing there—ten times better than silver—
    Is chiselling a girl who makes you quiver;
    The best thing in life is thrusting fast, it's fun,
    And striking the flint, before firing the gun.

Here's a hairy pit, until you get tired, Dafydd,
       To tame your prick;
       Here's a seat for your plums,
       Here you are, if you find the arse.

I'll come to you, sincere love, young man,
       Despise what is not to be seen.
       I'll follow you if I'm not held back,
       Brave noble lad with the long cock.

Best, nine times better than silver money,
       Is chiselling a fair lusty maid;
       The best thing in life is thrusting fast
       And the striking, before firing the cannon.

## 10. Dafydd Llwyd yn ateb Gwerful Mechain[1]

*Gwerful Mechain*

Cei bydew blew cyd boed blin—ei addo
    Lle gwedde dy bidin;
    Ti a gei gadair i'th eirin,
    A hwde o doi hyd y din.

*Dafydd Llwyd*

Cal felen rethren i ruthro—tewgont,
    A dwygaill amrosgo,
    Fel dyna drecs o dôn' ar dro
    A wnâi'r agen yn ogo'.

✪ ✪ ✪

## 10. Dafydd Llwyd replies to Gwerful Mechain

*Gwerful Mechain*

For all your moans you'll get a furry pit—I swear
    Where your penis will fit;
    You'll get a place for your plums to sit,
    And plenty of thatch up as far as your rear.

*Dafydd Llwyd*

I'll have a gold spear to make you behave—fat cunt,
    And the two balls of a giant,
    That's how my tackle will make you pliant,
    Transforming your little slit into a huge cave.

---

1   *Dafydd Llwyd yn ateb Gwerful Mechain*   These two *englynion* are to be found in one manuscript, namely the National Library of Wales 3039B (Mostyn 131), 109.

# 10. Dafydd Llwyd replies to Gwerful Mechain[1]

*Gwerful Mechain*

You'll get a hairy pit as long as you're tiresome—you're promised it
    Where your penis would fit;
    You'll get a seat for your plums,
    And plenty of thatch up as far as your arse.

*Dafydd Llwyd*

To have a yellow spear to attack—a fat cunt,
    And two giant balls,
    That's how the tackle will get twisted
    And makes the slit into a cave.

---

1   *Dafydd Llwyd replies to Gwerful Mechain*   This is another exchange of erotic *englynion* between the two poets. Note that Gwerful's *englyn* is very similar to the second stanza of her reply in the "Ymddiddan" (poem no. 9 above). The poems are humorous boasts about the excellence of the speakers' respective genitals.

# 11. I'w gŵr am ei churo[1]

Dager drwy goler dy galon—ar osgo
  I asgwrn dy ddwyfron;
Dy lin a dyr, dy law'n don,
A'th gleddau i'th goluddion.

❀ ❀ ❀

# 11. To her husband for beating her

A dagger through your heart's stone—on a slant
  To reach your breast bone;
May your knees break, your hands shrivel
And your sword plunge in your guts to make you snivel.

---

1   *I'w gŵr am ei churo*   There are 6 copies of this *englyn* in the manuscripts, located in the
British Library and the National Library of Wales.

# 11. To her husband for beating her[1]

A dagger through the collar of your heart—on a slant
   To the bone of your chest;
   Your knee breaks, your hand peels,
   And your weapons to your entrails.

---

1  *To her husband for beating her*  This is a heartfelt curse by a wife upon a violent husband
who has beaten her. It is impossible to know whether Gwerful herself was a victim of do-
mestic violence; it may be that, as she does elsewhere, she is speaking up for women more
generally. The succinct *englyn* form lends itself to the expression of an angry, bitter curse
such as this. It is interesting also to note the extremely physical emphasis of the poem, which
refers to the man's heart, breastbone, hands, knees, and guts but not his genitals; discus-
sion of those seems confined to Gwerful's more joyous and erotic explorations of human
relationships.

## 12. Gwlychu pais[1]

Fy mhais a wlychais yn wlych—a'm crys
    A'm cwrsi sidangrych;
    Odid Gwŷl Ddeinioel foelfrych
    Na hin Sain Silin yn sych.

❁ ❁ ❁

## 12. Wetting my petticoat

I got my petticoat wet and manky—and my shirt's
    Soaked and my wrinkly satin hanky;
    I'll still be drenched by St. Deiniol's Day, no lie,
    Nor even by St. Silin's will I be high and dry.

---

1   *Gwlychu pais*  There are 7 copies of this *englyn* in the manuscripts, located in the British Library and the National Library of Wales.

# 12. Wetting my petticoat[1]

My petticoat I wetted wet—and my shirt
    And my folded satin kerchief;
Not until speckled, tonsured St. Deiniol's Day[2]
    Nor St. Silin's good weather dry.[3]

---

1  *Wetting my petticoat*  This lively *englyn* describes how the speaker gets soaking wet and despairs of ever getting her clothes dry again. She refers to two saints' days in early September, both of which appear to have been associated with bad weather. Just as we still retain a superstition about St. Swithin's day (July 15) in contemporary Britain (if it rains on St. Swithin's it will continue to rain for another 40 days and nights), so it may be that St. Deiniol and St. Silin had similarly gloomy connotations in medieval Wales. Indeed, Nerys Ann Howells suggests that there may have been some confusion between Silin and Swithin (see Howells, op. cit., p. 170).

    The poem draws attention to its female speaker because of its precise reference to a petticoat and a satin kerchief (as well as to a shirt, which could be worn by either sex). The tone suggests that the speaker is annoyed at having perhaps ruined some favourite articles of clothing.

2  *St. Deiniol's Day*  St. Deiniol's Day is on the 11th of September. Deiniol (d. 584) is thought to have been the first Bishop of Bangor, in Gwynedd, North Wales.

3  *St. Silin's*  There are several early Celtic saints named Silin (or Sulien), associated with Cornwall, Britanny, and Wales; the one referred to here is probably the one associated with Britanny, whose feast day is on the 1st of September. Both Wrexham and Llansilin have churches dedicated to Saint Silin.

## 13. Llanc ym min y llwyn[1]

Rhown fil o ferched, rhown fwyn—lances,
    Lle ceisiais i orllwyn,
    Rhown gwŷn mawr, rhown gan morwyn
    Am un llanc ym min y llwyn.

❀ ❀ ❀

## 13. A lad beside the bush

I'd give a sweet plain jane, or a thousand damsels,
    As I kick my heels in vain,
    I'd give all my great lust, a hundred maidens,
    To have one strong lad beside this bush again.

---

1  *Llanc ym min y llwyn*  One copy of this *englyn* exists, in the National Library of Wales 1553ª, 694. The text is followed by the name "gwerfvl mechen" (sic).

## 13. A lad beside the bush[1]

I'd give a thousand girls, I'd give gentle—a damsel,
    Where I tried to wait,
    I'd give a great moan, I'd give a hundred maidens
For one lad beside the bush.

---

1   *A lad beside the bush*   This is another lively erotic *englyn* which expresses female sexual desire. Unlike the exchanges with Dafydd Llwyd, this *englyn* is not explicitly bawdy but instead expresses in a hyperbolic manner how much the female speaker longs to have just one young man alongside her "beside the bush." The rustic, sylvan setting is reminiscent of the "*deildy*" (house of leaves) in the works of Dafydd ap Gwilym, where lovers conduct their trysts.

## 14. I'w morwyn wrth gachu[1]

Crwciodd lle dihangodd ei dŵr—'n grychiast
    O grochan ei llawdwr;
    Ei deudwll oedd yn dadwr',
    Baw a ddaeth, a bwa o ddŵr.

�֍ �֍ ✖

## 14. To her maid as she shits

She squats and lets out her water—cascading
    From the cauldron of her pants as she totters;
    Her twin holes make a great bubbling clamour
    Then comes the dung and a rainbow arch of water.

---

1   *I'w morwyn wrth gachu*  Three copies of this *englyn* exist—in the National Library of Wales, in the Cwrt Mawr collection, and in the Peniarth collection.

## 14. To her maid as she shits[1]

She squatted where her water escaped—cascading
    From the cauldron of her pants;
    Her two holes bubbling
    Dirt came, and a bow of water.

1   *To her maid as she shits*  This scatological *englyn*, as Ceridwen Lloyd-Morgan notes, bears testimony to the serendipidous nature of the survival of an author's oeuvre. It is clearly a *jeu d'esprit* but also demonstrates the incorrigibly inventive nature of strict-metre poets of the middle ages. Literally any subject could provide them with a poetic challenge. Here, Gwerful rises to that challenge with characteristic verve (though one cannot help feeling a little sorry for the poor maid whose privacy has been so unceremoniously transgressed).

# POEMS OF
# UNCERTAIN AUTHORSHIP

(A rhymed, free translation appears
directly below the original medieval Welsh,
with a literal translation and
explanatory notes on the facing page.)

## 15. Ynghylch ei thad[1]

Howel Fychan o Gaer Gai ac ef ddim yn iach a ddanfonodd ei
ferch Gwerful Mechain i gymanfa yn ei le ac yn ei thŷ llety daeth
dynes i holi am Howel Fychan; hithau a ofynnodd ei gweled ac a
ddywedodd wrthi:

Gŵr penwyn sydyn at siad—findenau
    Adwaenir drwy'r hollwlad,
    Gŵr penllwyd o grap anllad,
    Gŵr edwyn hŵr ydyw 'nhad.

Gwedi ei dyfod yn ôl, ei thad a ofynnodd pa fodd y bu a pha beth
a welodd; hithau a atebodd:

Gweles eich lodes lwydwen—eiddilaidd,
    Hi ddylai gael amgen;
    Hi yn ei gwres, gynheswen,
    Chwithau 'nhad aethoch yn hen.

✿ ✿ ✿

## 15. About her father

Howel Fychan from Caer Gai being unwell sent his daughter
Gwerful Mechain to a meeting in his stead and in the lodging
house a woman came to ask for Howel Fychan; she asked to see
him and Gwerful said to her:

My white-haired old dad dallies with a thin-lipped girl:
    For this he's known throughout the world.
    A greybeard with a randy nature,
    My father's famed for bad behaviour.

When she returned, Gwerful's father asked her how things had
gone and what she had seen; she answered him:

I saw your dove-white girl—tender,
    Dad, she deserves better;
    She's in her heat, a white hot tidbit,
    And face it, father, you're long past it.

---

1  *Ynghylch ei thad*  This work is found in two manuscript copies, namely the National Library of Wales 436B, 104 and Peniarth 203, 137. Both are followed by an attribution to Gwerful Mechain.

# 15. About her father[1]

Howel Fychan from Caer Gai being unwell sent his daughter
Gwerful Mechain to a meeting in his stead and in the lodging
house a woman came to ask for Howel Fychan; she asked to see
him and Gwerful said to her:

A man whose hair has suddenly gone white goes to a thin-lipped jade
    Known throughout the land,
  A grey-haired man with a randy disposition,
  A man with a troublesome whore is my father.

When she returned, Gwerful's father asked her how things had
gone and what she had seen; she answered him:

I saw your grey-white girl—soft,
    She deserves better;
  She's in her heat, white hot,
  You, father, have got old.

---

1  *About her father*  This is a work of uncertain authorship, although its accompanying prose
explanation attributes it unmistakably to Gwerful Mechain. Ceridwen Lloyd-Morgan
points out that a similar poem is attributed to a later female poet, Alis ferch Gruffudd ap
Ieuan ap Llywelyn Fychan, in the Cwrtmawr manuscript, 25A, p. 4. (See Ceridwen Lloyd-
Morgan, "'Gwerful ferch rhagorol fain': Golwg newydd ar Gwerful Mechain," *Ysgrifau
Beirniadol* XVI (1990) pp. 94–95). It may be that Alis was consciously echoing Gwerful,
or simply that the theme of condemning an old man's taking a young wife is common in
women's poetry. Once again, it is not known whether Gwerful's father actually did take a
younger wife, or whether she is here speaking up for daughters of elderly men more gener-
ally. On these *englynion* see also Kathryn Curtis et al., "Beirdd benywaidd yng Nghymru
cyn 1800," *Y Traethodydd* CXLI (January, 1986) 18.

# 16. Pwy a gâr fwyaf?[1]

*Dafydd ab Edmwnd*

Ofnhau yr wyf yn fy nhyb
O ddal ar serch ddolur Siob,
O eiriau nwyf a ŵyr neb,
Ai cymaint serch merch â mab?

*Gwerful Mechain*

Cywirais ddydd, cerais ddoe
Cwyr dan sêl cariad a sai',
Clwyf ail modd, clyw fal y mae:
Cymaint yw serch merch a mwy.

✿ ✿ ✿

# 16. Who loves more passionately?

*Dafydd ab Edmwnd*

My thoughts go round, I rack my brain,
Will love just bring me Job's pain?
Tell me someone in the know who can:
Does a woman love as much as a man?

*Gwerful Mechain*

I loved once before and so can your fears dispel:
True love is stamped forever like a waxen seal,
It's another kind of pain: hark, then, to what I feel:
Woman's love is like man's, but it can his excel.

---

1 *Pwy a gâr fwyaf?* There are 17 copies (with some textual variations) of this exchange of *englynion*. The manuscripts are to be found in the University of Bangor, the British Library, Cardiff Central Library, and the National Library of Wales.

## 16. Who loves more passionately?[1]

*Dafydd ab Edmwnd*

In my thoughts I'm getting worried
About catching from love Job's[2] pain,
From words of passion, does anyone know,
Is a woman's love as great as a man's?

*Gwerful Mechain*

I correct today, I loved yesterday
Love will remain like a seal on wax,
Another kind of wound, listen to how it is:
A woman's love is as great or greater still.

---

1 *Who loves more passionately?* These two poems are attributed to Dafydd ab Edmwnd and Gwerful Mechain in several manuscript sources, though they remain anonymous in the majority of manuscripts. Dafydd ab Edmwnd and Gwerful Mechain were certainly contemporaries; the former was primarily known as a love poet, while Gwerful was renowned for her defence of women, so it would make sense for a question and answer about the relative capacities of men and women to love to come from Dafydd and Gwerful, respectively.

2 *Job* Job is an Old Testament prophet whose unmerited sufferings are proverbial.

## 17. Gwerful yn ateb Dafydd Llwyd[1]

*Dafydd Llwyd*

Os ceffyl cul, coeliwch—y feinir,
    A fynych farchogwch,
    Tost a chaled gochelwch
    Hallt a blin yw hollti blwch.

*Gwerful Mechain*

Ni hyllt naws gwyllt yn oes Gwen—galchw ...
    Fo amgylchwyd y fargen;
    ...e gïau'n ôl ar ei ddolen,

❁ ❁ ❁

## 17. Gwerful replies to Dafydd Llwyd

*Dafydd Llwyd*

Your nag is narrow and thin, believe me—my girl
    If you ride him out so free,
    Beware, your privates will hurt to the nth degree,
    And in the end it'll split your box, I guarantee.

*Gwerful Mechain*

Listen, a wild girl's nature does not split—your eyewash
    Means nothing—I will sit,
    Like a queen on my noble steed:
    The sinews on my ring are strong as steel.

---

1  *Gwerful yn ateb Dafydd Llwyd*  This unfinished exchange of *englynion* exists in one manuscript in the National Library of Wales, namely Peniarth 198, xiii.

# 17. Gwerful replies to Dafydd Llwyd[1]

*Dafydd Llwyd*

If the horse is narrow, believe me—the girl
 And you ride often,
 Beware, (you'll be) painful and hard
 Salty and wearisome is to split a box.

*Gwerful Mechain*

A wild nature does not split in Gwen's lifetime—whitewashed?
 The bargain is accomplished;
 …sinews back on his ring,

---

1  *Gwerful replies to Dafydd Llwyd*   In the manuscript Peniarth 198, xiii, these two poems are attributed to Gwerful Mechain and Dafydd Llwyd. The first *englyn* here is glossed with the explanation that it is the work of Dafydd Llwyd ap Llywelyn ap Gruffudd when he met "Gwerfŷl o Aber Tanat" on horseback riding through the river Tanat. Again, this appears to be a lighthearted exchange of bawdy *englynion* between the two poets, though Gwerful's *englyn* is incomplete in the manuscript. Dafydd is playfully warning Gwerful that she might do herself an injury by riding astride such a thin and decrepit horse. It is hard to guess what Gwerful's retort might have been but the tone is certainly dismissive of Dafydd's warning. I have provided a very free translation to indicate what Gwerful *may* have been saying.

## 18. Yr eira[1]

Gwynflawd, daeargnawd, du oergnu—mynydd,
    Manod wybren oerddu;
    Eira'n blât, oer iawn ei blu,
    Mwthlan a roed i'm methlu.

Eira gwyn ar fryn fry—a'm dallodd,
    A'm dillad yn gwlychu;
    O, Dduw gwyn, nid oedd genny'
    Obaith y down byth i dŷ.

❁ ❁ ❁

## 18. The snow

White flour, earthflesh, black mountain—with cold fleece
    Cold, black, snow-laden horizon;
    A plate of snow, feathers frozen,
    A soft snare to trip me all of a sudden.

White snow on a high peak blinded me,
    And my clothes were soaked;
    I really thought I'd never manage,
    Oh dear God, to reach the village.

---

1  *Yr eira*  These two *englynion* are found in 8 manuscript copies, located in Cardiff Central Library, and the National Library of Wales. Two of the manuscripts cite Gwerful Mechain as the author.

## 18. The snow[1]

White flour, earth flesh, cold black fleece—a mountain
 Fine snow cold black horizon;
 Snow a plate, very cold its feathers
 Soft thing given to trap me.

White snow on a high hill—that blinded me,
 And my clothes were getting wet;
 Oh, white God, I didn't have
 Hope that I'd ever come to a house.

---

1   *The snow*   In one manuscript this poem is glossed with an explanation that Gwerful, in
    returning home over the mountain from Trawsfynydd in the dead of winter, was overtaken
    by a snowstorm. She lost her way for some time and after finding it again she said this (the
    poems). See Cwrtmawr ms. 117, 211. The two *englynion* are examples of the poet's powers
    of *dyfalu* in that the snow is described in a series of inventive ways. The stanzas create a dra-
    matic situation, in which the speaker fears that the snow will prevent her from ever finding
    her way home, in an extremely succinct and immediate manner.

## 19. Y bedd[1]

Och! lety, gwely gwaeledd—anniddan
    Anheddle i orwedd,
    Cloëdig, unig annedd,
    Cas gan bawb yw cwsg y bedd.

❁ ❁ ❁

## 19. The grave

Oh last lodging, affliction's enclave,
    Hard abode to abide in; none craves
    To lie down in this locked, lonely cave,
    Nor longs for the sad sleep of the grave.

---

1   *Y bedd*  This *englyn* survives in one manuscript, namely Cwrtmawr 117, 211, in the National Library of Wales. It is followed by the note "Gwerfil a'i Cant" (Gwerful sang it).

## 19. The grave[1]

Oh! lodging, bed of illness—comfortless
　　Dwelling place to lie down in,
　　Locked, lonely dwelling,
　　Everyone hates the sleep of the grave.

---

1　*The grave*　This is a striking *englyn* describing the grave, our final resting place, as a lodging, a bed, a dwelling, a prison; its emphasis is on the lonely finality of that place. There is no religious consolation here. Nerys Howells points out the stylistic similarities to the early fifteenth-century poet Siôn Cent's well-known poem "I wagedd ac oferedd y byd" ("On the emptiness and vanity of the world").

# IN CONTEXT

## 20. I Anni Goch[1]

Merddin Wyllt am ryw ddyn wyf
Mewn oed anghymen ydwyf.
Awr ymhell yr amhwyllai,
Awr o'i gof gan Dduw ry gâi.
Minnau ni ddaw am unawr
Mewn y dydd na munud awr,
Ac ni chawn, gwen ni chwynai,
Gyty'r nos, gwatwar a wnâi,
A dwedyd, och nad ydwyf,
Anfad air, mai ynfyd wyf!

## 20. To Red Annie

I'm a man just like Merlin the Mad,
I'm foolish and my life's gone bad.
A long time ago he lost his wits,
God cursed him and he fell to bits.
And me? I've no peace by night or day,
Not a single minute to steal away,
For when I had her, the girl didn't complain,
But after she mocked me and would not deign
To acknowledge me, oh I've been had,
Oh wicked word, for I am mad!

---

1   *I Anni Goch*   There are 61 manuscript copies of this *cywydd*, each with some variations.
    The manuscripts are held in the University of Bangor, the British Library, Cardiff Central
    Library, and the National Library of Wales.

# Ieuan Dyfi, "I Anni Goch"

Ieuan Dyfi (fl. late 15th century) was a poet and contemporary of Gwerful Mechain, probably from Aberdyfi in Merionethshire, who wrote in the *cywydd* form. This *cywydd* is both a highly conventional and a deeply personal complaint againt women, in the misogynistic European tradition of the "querelles des femmes." For a scholarly account of this tradition, see Ceridwen Lloyd-Morgan, "The 'Querelle des Femmes': A Continuing Tradition in Welsh Women's Literature," in *Medieval Women: Texts and Contexts in Late Medieval Britain: Essays for Felicity Riddy* eds. Jocélyn Wogan-Browne et al. (Turnhout: Brepols, 2000) pp. 101–14. In this poem Ieuan Dyfi complains of his mistreatment by Anni Goch, and offers a sequence of exempla showing how great men have always been abused by deceitful women. Thanks to the scholarship of Llinos Beverley Smith, we know from court records of the time that Ieuan Dyfi and Annie Goch were indeed lovers, had up before the judges on more than one occasion for the sin of adultery (since Annie was married to one John Lippard). Ieuan received the punishment of six lashes, but Annie initially pleaded not guilty. Later, she was accused of plotting to kill her husband, and then she changed her plea, claiming that her husband had sold her to Ieuan Dyfi. Gwerful Mechain responds passionately to this poem, in defence of Annie Goch, and women in general (see no. 6 above).

## 20. To Red Annie

I am a man just like Wild Merlin,[1]
I'm at a foolish stage in my life.
A long time ago he lost his senses,
He got an hour of madness from God.
I get no peace in the day
Not a single minute,
And I didn't have her, the maiden didn't complain,
At night, she mocked me,
And said, woe is me that I am not,
Wicked word, that I am mad!

---

1  *Wild Merlin*  The poets of the period regarded the legendary Merlin as a prophet, madman, and lover. All these facets are reflected in the voice of the poet as he compares himself to Merlin.

Ni chaf forwyn o'i chyfryw,
Na farned gwen, fry nid gwiw.
Y cryfion gwychion a gaid,
Y dewrion benaduriaid,
Y doethion wedi hwythau
Agos i wraig â'u sarhau.
Samson, greulon gwroliaeth,
O dwyll ei wraig, dall yr aeth.
Pan oedd nod ei phriodas,
Y gŵr ei gryfder a gas;
E dynnodd yn oed unawr
Y llys ar ei wartha' i'r llawr.
Dyn wy' fwy-fwy dan fy ofn,
Dyn gwael wyf dan y golofn.
Selyf a droes, ail wyf draw,
Siom gwraig sy i'm gorugaw.
Alecsander, faner faith,
Bu dano y byd unwaith;

A maiden she was without equal,
And yet, for me, she turned out lethal.
But I'm not the only one who's ever been duped
Many great strong men have to women stooped,
Brave noblemen, sages, leaders of men
Have met disgrace because of women.
Great Samson, virile and strong,
Was blinded by his wife's wrong.
She had weaseled out the secret
Of his strength through sheer deceit,
And then he pushed the pillars down
The temple fell on their heads and on his own.
I'm a man like him increasingly afraid,
I'm a bad man standing in the pillars' shade.
Then there's Solomon of old, I'm like him too,
He who was conquered by a conjugal shrew.
Alexander the Great, whose flag unfurled
In majesty over the whole wide world;

I will not have a maiden her equal,
Don't judge the girl bad, from above.
Great stalwart ones have there been,
Brave noblemen,
Wise men have themselves
Been disgraced because of a woman.
Samson,[1] cruel manliness,
Went blind because of his wife's trickery.
The purpose of her marriage,
Was to get the secret of her husband's strength;
And then he pulled at that time
The court down upon them all.
I am a man increasingly afraid,
I am a bad man under the column.
I am like Solomon[2] of old,
Who was conquered by a wife's deceit.
Alexander,[3] great banner,
Who ruled the whole world once;

---

1 *Samson* Samson was one of the leaders of the Israelites in the Old Testament who was renowned for his extraordinary, God-given strength. The secret of his strength lies in his long hair; Delilah, a Philistine woman with whom Samson falls in love, manages to wheedle his secret out of him. She then cuts his hair while he sleeps and he is taken prisoner by the Philistines. Finally, after his eyes are put out and he is humiliated by his captors, he wreaks revenge on them by pulling down the walls of the temple upon them all as they worship their false god, Dagon. See Judges 16.28–30.

2 *Solomon* Solomon was the son of David and King of Israel, renowned for his wealth and wisdom. However, he took several wives and, according to I Kings 11.4, they succeeded in turning him away from the true God to worship foreign idols.

3 *Alexander* Alexander the Great (356–323 BCE) was a King of Macedon who came to rule, through successful military campaigns and conquests, over one of the most extensive empires of the ancient world. Gwerful Mechain also refers to Alexander in "To Llywelyn ap Gutun" (poem no. 5 above).

Nid âi ungwr â'i deyrnged,
Ond tent gwraig, tu hwnt i Gred.
Aristotlus, gweddus gwir,
A dwyllwyd o deallir;
Yntau yn fodd, hwnt yn faith,
A'i talodd ati eilwaith;
Am ei thwyll a wnaeth allan,
I eiliw'r tes olau'r tân.
Ipo gynt anap a gâi,
Ac un wen a'i gwenwynai;
Aeth o'i gyngor y forwyn
I'r llech oer, llai fu ei chŵyn.
Siason i ddynion oedd dda,
Siom adewis Medeia:
Cur tost fu eu cariad hwy,
Cwrs mawr fal Cruwsa 'm murwy.
Ni wn wenwyn un annerch,
Na chas mwy no cheisio merch.

Tribute was paid him by every nation,
But he was laid low by a woman's temptation.
Aristotle, worthy and true,
Was deceived, we believe, by a minx who,
Offended, managed to get him to pay
By riding on his back, sad to say,
For her trickery quenched his rational light
Like the burning haze of firelight.
Old Hippocrates, father of medicine,
Was laid in the earth by the poison
His fair wife gave him; he took her advice
And went where her nagging was less.
A good man was Jason, until he left
Medea, who was vengeful and bereft;
Their love was a painful horror
Leaving Creusa to die in torture.
But there's no poison worse than wooing:
Chasing a girl's every man's undoing.

Not one man would fail to pay tribute,
But a woman's temptation, beyond Christendom.
Aristotle,[1] proper and true,
As we understand, was deceived;
He was a means, beyond all reason,
For her to get her own back;
For her trickery he went out,
Like the warm haze of firelight.
Hippocrates[2] of yore came to grief,
A fair one poisoned him;
He went on the maiden's advice
To the cold slate, where her complaint was less.
Jason[3] was held to be good by men,
Disappointed he left Medea:[4]
A painful affliction was their love,
A great trouble like Creusa[5] in fetters.
I don't know of any poison worse than pursuing,
Nothing worse than trying to win a girl.

---

1  *Aristotle*  Aristotle, the Greek philosopher (384–322 BCE), was Alexander's tutor when the latter was a boy. An apocryphal story tells of Aristotle warning the Young Alexander against the wiles of women; he is overheard by a courtesan, Phyllis, who sets about seducing and humbling the great Aristotle. She does so by making him fall in love with her and forcing him to allow her to ride him like a horse. Alexander witnesses this and is angry with his tutor, but Aristotle turns the humiliation to his own advantage by stating that the fact that a great philosopher like himself can be tricked by a woman demonstrates their guile and treachery.

2  *Hippocrates*  Hippocrates (460–370 BCE), generally regarded as "'the Father of Medicine," was poisoned by his wife, according to legend.

3  *Jason*  Jason was a hero in Greek mythology, leader of the Argonauts, who retrieved the Golden Fleece. Here, though, he represents a man betrayed by a woman, since he abandoned his lover, Medea (see below) and was punished by her when she killed their two children, and his new bride, Creusa. See Euripedes' tragedy, *Medea*.

4  *Medea*  Medea was the daughter of King Aeetes of Colchis, niece of Circe and granddaughter of the sun god, Helios. She helped Jason retrieve the Golden Fleece from her father's kingdom. In mythology and literature she is depicted as a powerful sorceress.

5  *Creusa*  Creusa (also known as Glauce) in Greek mythology was the daughter of King Creon of Corinth. She was given a poisoned robe and crown by Medea (see above) which, when she put them on, stuck to her body and killed her. Thus did Medea avenge Jason's abandoning of her and their children in favour of Creusa.

Am Elen fu'r gynnen gynt,
Oes Droea a ddistrywynt.
Achos gwên Policsena
Llas o dwyll Achilles da.
Eneas wyf yn nwyawr
Wedi'r farn ar Droea fawr.
Un alar er a wnelwyf
Â Brutus ap Sulys wyf
Wedi lladd, deall yddyn',
Ei fam a'i dad, wyf â'm dyn.
Ercles, ni wedes, ydwyf,
Och o'r serch, un echrys wyf,
Neu Baris, wyneb oerwynt,
Ofnog oedd am Feian gynt.
Gwraig a wnaeth hil Groeg yn wan,
Gwaed ac ymliw'r Gad Gamlan.
Gwraig Fadog fwyn o Wynedd,

❈ ❈ ❈

Look at Helen—the cause of that old conflict,
And because of her great Troy is derelict.
And it was for Polixena's smile,
That Achilles died, through a woman's guile.
I'm like Aeneas in the two long hours
That came in the wake of the fall of Troy's towers.
The pain that afflicts me is equally grievous
As Aeneas' great grandson, Brutus, son of Silvius,
Who mistakenly killed both his father and mother,
As the seer predicted: they perished together.
I'm also like Hercules, forgot to mention,
A slave to love, maimed by his obsession.
Or like Paris, exposed as a babe on a hill,
So fearful of Venus he carried out her will.
A woman it was who marred the grandeur of Greece,
A woman it was who caused Merlin's decease.
The sickly sweet wife wrought prince Madog's shame,

The old dispute was over Helen,[1]
And because of her Troy was destroyed.
Because of Polixena's[2] smile,
Good Achilles was killed through treachery.
I am like Aeneas in the two hours
After the judgement on great Troy.
The grief that I have is like
That of Brutus,[3] son of Silvius,
After the death of his mother and father,
When he learnt that, I am like him.
I haven't said yet, I'm also like Hercules,[4]
Suffering from love, injured I am,
Or like Paris,[5] face in a cold wind,
Fearful he was of Venus long ago.
It was a woman who weakened the lineage of Greece,
The blood and rebuke of the Battle of Camlan.[6]
The gentle wife of Madog,[7] she from Gwynedd,

---

1   *Helen*   Helen was the daughter of Zeus and Leda, and figures in Greek mythology as the
    most beautiful of mortal women. She was married to King Menelaus of Sparta; her elopement
    with the Trojan Prince, Paris, gave rise to the Trojan war, narrated by Homer in the *Iliad*.
2   *Polixena*   Polixena was the youngest daughter of King Priam and Queen Hecuba of Troy.
    According to some tales, it was she who found out the secret of Achilles' vulnerability and
    who lured him to a temple, where her surviving brother, Paris, killed Achilles by shooting
    an arrow into his heel.
3   *Brutus*   Brutus (of Troy) was the great grandson of Aeneas and the legendary founder of
    Britain, which is named after him, according to Geoffrey of Monmouth in his *Historia
    Regum Britanniae* (1136). It was prophesied that Brutus, rather like Oedipus, would inad-
    vertently slay his own parents; this story is recounted both by Geoffrey of Monmouth and
    in the earler *Historia Brittonum* by Nennius. He was banished as a result and his wanderings
    finally brought him to the Island of Britain.
4   *Hercules*   Hercules (or Herakles) was a Greek and Roman mythological hero, son of Zeus
    and Alcmene, famed for his strength and his many great exploits, including the legendary
    "Twelve Labours." Presumably here the allusion is to the tale of his wife, Deianira, who gives
    him a shirt soaked in the blood of the centaur Nessus, thinking that it will keep him faithful
    to her. But the centaur's blood is tainted and when Hercules dons the "shirt of Nessus" it
    kills him.
5   *Paris*   Paris was one of the sons of King Priam and Queen Hecuba of Troy. He eloped with
    Helen, wife of Menelaus, causing the Trojan War. When he was a baby, this catastrophic
    action was foretold, so that he was exposed on the mountainside to die, but he survived and
    fulfilled his destiny.
6   *the Battle of Camlan*   The Battle of Camlan was, according to legend, the battle in which
    Merlin was either killed or mortally wounded by Mordred, who also perished there.
7   *Madog*   Madog is probably a reference to Madog ap Maredudd of Powys, whose wife was
    from Gwynedd, but the story referred to here concerning them remains obscure.

Gwn a wnaeth, mae gwen un wedd.
Ofydd, drosof oedd draserch,
Fryd Sylus wyf, frad sêl serch.
Merddin aeth, mawrddawn ei wedd,
Mewn gwydr er mwyn ei gydwedd;
Nid aeth, oedd adwyth iddi,
Y drws o'i hôl a droes hi.
Aeth y rhain, waith rhianedd,
Yn feirwon, wyf yr un wedd.
Ni bu Dduw heb ei ddial,
Ni wyddiad hon na ddaw tâl.
Myn y Wir Grog, mannau'r Groes,
Minnau fynnaf, myn f'einioes,
Ai'i lladd hi, oni'm lludd hon,
Ai'i chael o fodd ei chalon.

❂ ❂ ❂

I know what she did: women are all the same.
Ovid, like me, was smitten by passion,
And Silvius, too, betrayed in like fashion.
The gifted great Merlin at his lover's behest
Went into the glass house on the isle in the west
But she didn't follow, damned be her eyes,
She closed the door behind her, and there he still lies.
All these great men lost their lives
To heartless women and their wiles.
But God will not fail to punish their sin
This woman, I swear it, will fail to win.
Jesus will triumph, by the stations of the Cross,
And I too insist that her life will be no loss
For I'll kill her, if she doesn't prevent me,
And thus at last our hearts will united be.

I know what she did, women are all the same.
Ovid,[1] like me, was infatuated,
I am like Silvius,[2] my love sealed by treachery.
Merlin went, greatly gifted as he was,
Into a glass house[3] for his beloved's sake;
She didn't go, plague on her,
She closed the door behind her.
All these lost their lives because of
Women's work, and I'm the same as them.
God will not fail to seek vengeance,
This one doesn't know that she will be punished.
Christ insists on the truth, by the stations of the Cross,
I too insist, on my life,
I will kill her, if she doesn't prevent me,
And will thus win her heart at last.

---

1  *Ovid*  Ovid (43 BCE–17/18 CE), Roman poet, author of the *Amores, Ars Amatoria,* and the *Metamorphoses.* He was especially renowned in the Middle Ages as the great poetic expert on affairs of the heart, which is why he is a point of reference in Ieuan Dyfi's *exempla.*
2  *Silvius*  Silvius, father of Brutus, who had an adulterous affair with the niece of Lavinia, daughter of King Latinus, who was Aeneas', his father's, second wife. Brutus was the result of this clandestine relationship.
3  *glass house*  The glass house features in two different guises in legends associated with Merlin. Firstly, it is a magic place of incarceration on Bardsey Island (*Ynys Enlli*), which Merlin's beloved, Viviane, tricks him into entering, and from which he is unable to escape. Secondly, it is a magic dwelling on the island to which Merlin goes voluntarily, taking with him the Thirteen Treasures of Britain and the True Throne of Arthur for safekeeping. Clearly, it is the first story that is alluded to here, indicating as it does the alleged perfidy and danger of women.

## 21. Cywydd llateiaeth i Werful Mechain ac i yrru Llywelyn ap Gutun ati yn llatai[1]

Claf wyf eisiau cael y ferch,
Dwyn unwaith i'm dyn annerch,
Gwerful, ferch ragorol fain
Hywel Fychan, haul Fechain.
Pa dir, gwn pwy a dyn wyd,
Pa le draw, pa wlad yr wyd?
Hwyliaist fal yn un helynt,
Gwn gof chwedl y fargen gynt,

❁ ❁ ❁

## 21. A love-message poem to Gwerful Mechain, sending Llywelyn ap Gutun to her as a messenger

I'm sick from trying to get the lass,
Just once to greet her but alas,
Gwerful, Hywel of Mechain's sweetie,
Slender and sassy, won't reply.
You're there somewhere but in what place,
What distant land, do you hide your face?
You left me in one heck of a strop,
The pact we made is for the chop.

---

1   *Cywydd llateiaeth ... yn llatai*   There are 41 manuscript copies of this poem, found in the University of Bangor, the British Library, Cardiff Central Library, and the National Library of Wales.

# Dafydd Llwyd, "Cywydd llateiaeth i Werful Mechain ac i yrru Llywelyn ap Gutun ati yn llatai"

This *cywydd* should be read in conjunction with Gwerful Mechain's "I Llywelyn ap Gutun" (no. 5 above) and Llywelyn ap Gutun's "Ateb i'r cywydd llateiaeth" (no. 22 below). Dafydd Llwyd here takes on the voice of the passionate lover who is languishing because of his failure to contact his beloved. The details of the separation between himself and Gwerful are unclear, but the need for stealth is apparent; for this reason he must send Llywelyn ap Gutun as a messenger to her on his behalf. The *llatai* (messenger) is a common device in Welsh medieval poetry and can take the form of an animal or bird or even an inanimate object, as well as another person. However, in this instance, Dafydd appears to have selected an incompetent *llatai* in the form of Llywelyn, who is no great walker and an indifferent poet, according to Dafydd. Indeed, he is only fulfilling this role because he has been beaten by Dafydd and must therefore obey him. As this synopsis suggests, the poem is a mixture of conventional love poem and *ad hominem* satire; both aspects, we may suspect, were intended simply to amuse the recipient, Gwerful Mechain, and to elicit from her a poem in response.

## 21. A love-message poem to Gwerful Mechain, sending Llywelyn ap Gutun to her as a messenger

I'm ill from trying to get the girl,
Give greeting once to the person,
Gwerful, excellent slim daughter of
Hywel Fychan, the sun of Mechain.[1]
What land, I know who you are,
What far place, in what country are you?
You set off like one in a strop,
I know by heart the story of the bargain we made,

---

1   *Hywel Fychan, the sun of Mechain*   Mechain or Llanfechain is a village in Powys (formerly Montgomeryshire), a sparsely-populated rural area in north-east Wales, not far from the border with England. Hywel Fychan was Gwerful's father; she is presumed to have been named after the place where she lived. It is north-east of Llwydiarth, where her father's family originated.

I adwedd ydd âi eidiawn,
Neu hydd gwyllt bonheddig iawn;
Er bwrw gwalch i'r wybr gylchoedd
E ddaw i'r un llaw ydd oedd.
Ni ddout ti rhag dy sbïaw
Led dy droed o'th lety draw.
Ni chawn dy gydfod, tro trig,
Mwy no didro Brawd Odrig,
Na pha fan y cawn d'annerch,
Na pha'r sir, ni phery serch.
Gollyngaist, gwall o angof,
Rai ar a'th garai o'th gof.
Gollwng, perhôn a'i golli,
A wnaf latai i'th dai di,
Ar draws llif, ag ysgrifen,
Brynhawn hwyr fal brân Noe hen.
Llywelyn gerdded-ddyn gwael
A ddanfonaf, ddyn feinael,

Every creature returns to its home,
A bullock or even a stag won't roam;
A goshawk turning in the widening gyre
Will fly back to the hand of his squire.
But you won't set a foot outside
Your house in case you are espied.
Finding you's a harder, longer trip
Than the fabled wanderings of Brother Odoric,
I just don't know where I can meet you,
Or where our love is, can I get through?
You set me loose from your mind,
The one who loves you, maiden unkind.
But I will set loose, and send to your house
A messenger; what if I lose the louse?
Across the river he'll come with my note,
Like old Noah's raven from the boat.
It's Llywelyn I'll send you, delicate one,
Lousy walker he is when all's said and done

A bullock goes back home,
Or a very noble wild stag;
Though a hawk be thrown into the air in circles
He will come back to the same hand that held him.
But you won't come in case you're spied
Out of your house by even one step.
I can't meet you, journey to your dwelling,
It's harder than the wandering of Brother Odoric,[1]
Nor do I know where I can greet you,
Nor in what county, nor will love survive.
You let go from your mind, mad oblivion,
Those ones who loved you.
I will let go, even if I lose him,
A love-messenger to your house,
Across the river, with a written message,
One late afternoon like old Noah's[2] raven.
Llywelyn a poor walker
Will I send, fine-browed woman,

1   *Odoric*   Odoric (c. 1286–1331) was an Italian Franciscan friar renowned for his wander-
    ings, which included a journey to China. He is also referred to in Gwerful's "I Llywelyn ap
    Gutun," no. 5 above.
2   *Noah*   Noah was the just man in the Old Testament who built an ark according to God's
    instructions in order to save the righteous and the animals from the great Flood sent by God
    to punish transgressive human beings. The story is told in Genesis, chapters 6–9. Noah is
    also mentioned in Gwerful's poem, "Angau a barn," no. 2 above.

Gŵr a fedr wrth roi dedryd,
Meddan', bedwar ban y byd.
Ceinioca bu'n gynta' gwaith,
Yta ac wyna ganwaith.
Ef a ddaw, er anfodd un,
Ag ateb, Fab y Gytun.
Diwydiach, felly dwedynt,
Fydd gwas wedi'i faeddu gynt.
Y cenau gyda'r cynydd,
Ei arfer, pan faedder, fydd
Caru'r meistr a'i curo
A'i ganlyn a fyn efô.
Fal hyn, Lywelyn lew iawn
Delynor heb awdl uniawn,
Ni bu wawdydd llonydd llwyd
Ufuddach er pan faeddwyd.
Ni fyn elw ond fy nilid,
Ar f'ôl, bol y baeol, bid.

But he is a man who has an opinion
On every corner of God's dominion.
Begging for pennies is his reputation,
Plus eating and sheep stealing across the nation.
Yes, Gutun's son, it's him who'll bring
Me your answer, though he be unwilling,
For the servant, they say, works twice as hard
After he's been thrashed by the angry bard.
Like the whelp with the huntsman
Is all the better when he's been beaten,
The more he's hit, the more he loves his master,
His goal in life is to follow him faster.
Just like this whelp is Llywelyn the shrewd,
A crude harpist without a proper ode.
There never was a still, grey mockingbird
More obedient than him ever since he was conquered.
He asks no reward except my mercy,
The one with the paunch always tags along with me.

A man who can pass judgement,
So they say, on the four corners of the world.
Begging for pennies was his first job,
Then eating and gathering lambs a hundred times.
He will bring, though he be unwilling,
An answer, Gutun's son.
As they say, more diligent
Will the servant be after he's been beaten.
The whelp with the huntsman,
When he is beaten, usually
Loves his master more, the more he is hit
And all he wants to do is follow him.
Just like this is very clever Llywelyn
A harpist without a proper ode,
There was never a still, grey mocker
More obedient ever since he was conquered.
He wants no profit except my mercy,
The pot-bellied one will always follow me.

## 22. Ateb i'r cywydd llateiaeth[1]

Cennad wyf a wna cynnen,
Os gwir hawg ysgwïer hen.
Harri a'i gwnaeth, dadmaeth da,
Bumed, hir y bu yma.
Trafael faith at Werful fain
Ddifai wych o ddwy Fechain,
Ac yno'n wir nis gwnâi'n un
 lloer olau llawr Alun,
A Dafydd, ben saethydd serch,
Yn henwr yn ei hannerch.
Duw a roes uwch daear wen

❁ ❁ ❁

## 22. A response to the love-message poem

I'm a messenger who likes to squawk,
Oh ancient squire, so like a hawk.
Your foster-dad, old Henry the Fifth
Lived a really long time, like all your kith.
I've had to beat a long hard path to lovely G,
That paragon of the two Mechains under the trees.
And sad to say she did not like the scene
With the moon shining on the waters of Alun,
For Dafydd who wooed her was no great Cupid
But a doddery ancient, daft and stupid.
He was around when God delivered

---

1 *Ateb i'r cywydd llateiaeth*   There are 39 copies of this *cywydd* in the manuscript sources, located in the University of Bangor, the British Library, Cardiff Central Library, and the National Library of Wales.

# Llywelyn ap Gutun, "Ateb i'r cywydd llateiaeth"

This is the satirical response by Llywelyn ap Gutun to Dafydd Llwyd's *cywydd* (no. 21 above), sending him as a love messenger to Gwerful Mechain. Llywelyn gets his own back for Dafydd's insulting description of him in that poem by emphasizing Dafydd's old age and decrepitude, suggesting that the lovely young Gwerful would have no interest in his approaches. Instead, Llywelyn suggests that he himself, being young like Gwerful, would woo her successfully. The tone of the poem is best understood as lighthearted and the insults exchanged should be read as part of the poetic contest, rather than as indicative of a serious rivalry. Nevertheless, Gwerful is certainly presented by both poets as a woman of beauty and wit, well worth the attempt to win over.

The last six lines of the poem are difficult to make any sense of; it is probable that a number of lines are missing.

## 22. A response to the love-message poem

I'm a messenger who makes discord,
If true old hawklike squire.
Harry did it, good foster-father,
The Fifth,[1] he was here for a long time.
A long travail toward slim Gwerful
Excellent faultless one from the two Mechains,[2]
And there truly she did not make one
With the moon shining on the valley floor of the Alun,[3]
With Dafydd, great archer of love,
An old man sending her greetings.
God brought down above the beautiful earth

---

1   *Harry ... The Fifth*   King Henry V of England (1386–1422). The dates indicate that Llywelyn is mocking Dafydd's extreme old age.

2   *two Mechains*   The two places are Mechain Is Coed and Mechain Uwch Coed ("beneath the wood" and "above the wood," respectively).

3   *the Alun*   There are several rivers called "Alun" in Wales; this one is likely to be the tributary of the river Dee in Clwyd, north-east Wales.

Draw ar ddyn dŵr Eurddonen.
Nid hŷn ei weled heno
Â ffon fawr, no phan fu fo
Yn y Bryn Glas, obry'n glain,
Yn ei law, yn ôl Owain.
Meddylgar yw am ddeilgoed,
Ac fal y plwm trwm yw'r troed.
Merched ac yfed a gâr
Marchog oediog, ac adar.
Edrych ar ferch wych uchod,
A chan ferch ni ddichon fod.
Er hyn nid gwiw, rhyw nâd gŵydd,
Edrych ar anynadrwydd.
Er ei fwyn i ddwyn ydd af
Yr ateb a roir ataf.
O dwedwn i air didwyll
Ni chredai nad âi yn dwyll.

✿ ✿ ✿

The Israelites from the Jordan river.
Tonight he looks no whit older and yet
He fought in Bryn Glas, embattled, beset,
With Owain, his spear in hand, nimble and quick,
But now that hand rests on a walking stick.
He dreams about sweet bowers of bliss,
But his feet are like lead; it's come to this.
He's an eye for women, this agèd knight,
And booze and birds, he's quite a sight.
He moons and stalks a lovely lass,
But after all, can't make a pass.
To watch a fool like that so long
Is jarring, like a goose's song.
At any rate I have to take him
˙ The answer I have, even if it shakes him.
The trouble is when I tell him the facts
He doubts me—that's just how he reacts.
But this time I really will play a trick,

Yonder on men the waters of Jordan.[1]
No older we see him tonight
Than when he was in Bryn Glas,[2]
With a great stick in his hand,
Beneath him a jewel, following Owain.[3]
Pensive he is about leafy trees,
And his feet are as heavy as lead.
He loves women and drinking
And birds, agèd knight.
He gazes at a lovely girl above,
But he is unable to be with a girl.
It's not pleasant, some goose's honk,
To witness such foolishness.
For his sake I'll go to carry
The answer I am given.
If I said a sincere word
He wouldn't believe that it was no trick.

---

1  *the waters of Jordan*  The Jordan is a river in the Middle East which has great symbolic significance in biblical narratives. It is the river crossed by the Israelites to enter the Promised Land, and also the river in which Christ was baptised. These lines may refer to the story narrated in Joshua 4 where the waters of the Jordan parted for the Israelites, just as the Red Sea had done for Moses (Exodus 13–14).

2  *Bryn Glas*  The Battle of Bryn Glas took place on June 22, 1402. It was a victory for Owain Glyndŵr (see note below) against the forces of the Marcher Lord, Edmund Mortimer. Enid Roberts suggests that this may be an accurate reference to Dafydd Llwyd's participation in the battle (see her *Dafydd Llwyd o Fathafarn*, 1981); however, it is likely that Dafydd was born some time later, in which case he could not have taken part. On that reading, this reference would form part of Llywelyn's exaggeration of Dafydd's old age.

3  *Owain*  Owain Glyndŵr (c. 1359–c.1415) was a Welsh Prince who waged a long-running but ultimately unsuccessful rebellion against the English. He appears as a character (Glendower) in Shakespeare's play, *Henry IV, Part 1*.

Er hyn o ffrost ar osteg,
Rhaid oedd geisio'i dwyllo'n deg.
Od af dan ddail haf â hi
Draw i Ddafydd drwy Ddyfi,
Pa ddiawl, pan na ddialwn,
Fy mod yn herod i hwn?
Neud hawdd ei ganfod heddiw
Oll yn llwyd megis Llyn Lliw,
Rhy brudd ydyw'r gradd a'r gran,
Rhyw awdr yn rhoi oedran.
Hynod fydd, hŷn ydyw fo,
Glog aur, no'r golwg arno:
Dwyflwydd, fel cledr y daflawd,
A chweugain aeth uwch ei gnawd!
Hŷn yw'r gŵr hwn no'r garreg,
Ac unoed wyf â gwen deg.
Oed am irgoed yw 'margen,
Ni wreiddia imp ar wraidd hen.

✿ ✿ ✿

All this messenger business just makes me sick.
It's time for me to get my vengeance
On Dafydd I shan't dance attendance,
For when I'm 'mid the leaves with her,
Goddamn, I'll be his slave no longer.
Today the world is hard to view
For all is grey just like Llyn Lliw,
And grey too are his skin and cheek,
Which gives away that he's antique.
It's strange, he's that much older
Than he looks, which makes me bolder;
Two years it took him to raise a roof girder
And his poor flesh is not worth a tenner!
The man is older than the rocks of this hill
And I'm the same age as the pretty *jeune fille*.
A date in a greenwood will end my pursuit
For a cutting won't take on a withered old root.

Despite this boasting in public,
I had to try to trick him thoroughly.
If I go under the summer leaves with her
Over there to Dafydd through Dyfi,
What devil, if I didn't retaliate,
That I'm a herald for him?
To make easy to find today
Everything's grey like Llyn Lliw,[1]
Too sad is the cheek and the face,
Some poet giving away his age.
It will be strange, he's older
Than he looks, golden skull:
Two years, like a roof beam,
And ten shillings went above his flesh!
This man is older than the rock,
And I'm the same age as the pretty girl.
A date in a verdant wood is my bargain,
A cutting won't take on an old root.

---

1   *Llyn Lliw*  Llyn Lliw is a lake mentioned in the medieval prose tale *Culhwch ac Olwen* in
    which there is an episode involving the hero asking advice and guidance from the most
    ancient animals in the world, including the salmon of Llyn Lliw. The reference is, once
    more, mocking Dafydd's extreme old age.

Celffaint o henaint yw hwn,
A gwreiddiog ac ir oeddwn.
A bryno hen fargen faith
Obry'n ôl a brŷn eilwaith.
Ni ŵyl dros donnau Alun
Ef ei haint na'i fai ei hun.
Ni chwarddodd Duw, chwerwddydd dwys,
Wrth hwnnw, arth o Wennwys,
Pan geisiawdd, er gwahawdd gwen,
Wisorwy was o Urien.

This man is an ancient shrunken stump,
While I am fruitful, sleek and plump.
For she who thinks she gets a second-hand bargain
Must take it back and buy new once again.
He weeps not over the waves of the Alun,
He's oblivious to his sickness and shame,
But God looked sadly down on this,
On him, the bear of Wennwys,
When he sought me, at a girl's invitation,
A sorrowful servant from Urien.

This man is a withered stump of old age,
And I am rooted and fruitful.
He who buys an old long bargain
Must take it back and buy a second time.
He will not weep over the waves of the Alun
His own sickness or his guilt.
God did not laugh, grave bitter day,
At him, the bear of Wennwys,[1]
When he sought, at a girl's invitation,
With sorrow a servant from Urien.[2]

---

1   *Wennwys*   Gwennwys was the son of Gruffudd ap Beli (b. 1132) of Montgomeryshire. The
    reference here and in the following lines, however, remains obscure.

2   *a servant from Urien*   This is probably a reference to Urien Rheged, a late sixth-century
    leader of the "Hen Ogledd" (Old North, the Brythonic territories of northern England
    and southern Scotland). The reference is obscure but appears to be in line with Llywelyn's
    emphasis on Dafydd's old age.

## 23. Moliant i Werful Mechain[1]

Gwnaeth ym fun faith anhunedd,
Gwerful wych, ragorol wedd:
Moddus yw dy gof, meddir,
Mechain hwyl, mae achwyn hir.
Anfon llateion 'dd wyt ti
I'm hannerch er 'y mhoeni,
Mawl a cherdd aml a chân
I'm twyllo o'm tŷ allan:
Nid felly, riain feinael,
Draw, er fy ngheisiaw, fy nghael!
Ffel wyf pan ganwyf i'r gog,
A di-wair a daueiriog.

✾ ✾ ✾

## 23. In praise of Gwerful Mechain

You, girl, have made me fail to fall asleep,
Your beauty, Gwerful, means that I'm in deep;
Your mind is lovely too, I'm glad to say,
You're the joyful spirit of Mechain from day to day.
However, I do have a bit of a grumble:
You keep sending messengers who come and mumble
And plague and annoy me with their poems and ditties
To trick me out of doors; it's a thousand pities.
So, sweetheart, let me tell you that's not the way
To get me to come, however much you try!
I'm a crafty old singer, just like the cuckoo,
I'm faithful but also can deceive one or two.

---

1 *Moliant i Werful Mechain* There are four extant copies of this *cywydd*, with many varia-
tions, in the manuscripts, located in the British Library, Cardiff Central Library, and the
National Library of Wales.

# Dafydd Llwyd, "Moliant i Werful Mechain"

This is a love poem addressed to Gwerful Mechain by Dafydd Llwyd. This time it is Gwerful who has been sending love messengers to Dafydd (unlike the situation in nos. 5, 21, and 22). It seems that Dafydd is somewhat coy, not liking the overt nature of Gwerful's approaches. He urges her to be more circumspect and expresses his desire to be with her in secret. The second half of the poem turns into a conventional celebration of love in the open air, in the shade of the birch grove; such material often appears in the love poems of medieval Wales.

## 23. In praise of Gwerful Mechain

The girl made me sleepless for a long time,
Lovely Gwerful, beautiful face:
Shapely is your mind, they say,
Mechain's good spirits, there's long grumbling.
You send love messengers
To greet and annoy me,
Many praise poems and songs
To trick me to come out of my house:
Not in that way, delicate browed maiden,
Will you get me to come, though you try!
Crafty am I when I sing to the cuckoo,
And faithful and deceitful.

Nid un ferch a adwen fu
Ardderchawg i'm gordderchu.
Nid awn er lliw gwawn i goed,
Ni'm cafas neb o'm cyfoed.
Ni'm twyllir, ddyn, meddir mwy,
Â gair medrus nac er modrwy.
Er hyn o sôn, lle rhown serch,
Gweirful wen, gŵyr fawl annerch,
Be'i celud, ryw hyd â hwn,
Gyfrinach a gyfrannwn,
Erod y down, aur dy dâl,
I Ffridd Ddeunaint, ffyrdd anial.
N'ad, wen, i liain d'wyneb
Wybod d'adnabod i neb.
Gwnawn ddydd, ac yno, ddeuddyn,
Ar y braich ar gwr y bryn,
Rhodio gwŷdd yn rhad a gawn,
Pob llannerch, pebyll uniawn,

Not one girl has managed to get the better of me
Not one smart girl has made me her devotee.
Nothing seduced me, not the gossamer on the trees,
No girl of my age ever made me her squeeze.
I won't be tricked by a girl, however skillful,
To give her a ring for love poems blissful.
But despite all this I would give you my love,
Dear Gwerful, and your greetings approve
If you agreed to make it more clandestine,
In secret we'll come together and we'll nest in
Deunaint Wood, where we'll come by lonely ways,
And there we'll embrace in our golden days.
Darling, keep the veil over your face
Don't let anyone recognize you, just in case.
We'll do it one day, the two of us there,
In a nook of the hill, entwined, with no care.
Freely we'll walk beneath the trees' shade,
The branches our canopy, glad in every glade.

Not one girl of my acquaintance has there been
Excellent to ravish me.
I wouldn't go for the colour of gossamer to the trees,
Not one girl of my age had me.
I won't be tricked, girl, more skillful,
With a metrical word nor for a ring.
Despite saying all this, where I would give my love,
Pretty Gwerful, praise and greetings I'd give,
If it were hidden, for as long as this,
In secret we'll exchange,
We will come together, gold your payment,
To Deunaint Wood, by deserted ways.
Darling, don't move the veil from your face
Don't let anyone recognize you.
We will do it one day, and there, the two of us,
Arm in arm in a nook of the hill,
We'll be able to walk beneath the trees freely,
In every glade, fair tents,

Cydymddiddan dan y dail,
Cydgerdded coed ac irddail;
Ymwasgu, ymgaru i gyd,
Â breichiau a bair iechyd.
Da waith oedd, heb adwyth hir,
Ddwylaw mwnwgl ddaly meinir.
Capel gwydr o'r mydr y mau
Yn ennaint a wnawn innau,
A gwely mewn y llwyn golas
Draw, rhag ein ceisiaw o'n cas,
A byw'n hir heb wayw na haint,
Heb boen arnom, heb henaint:
Ys da fyd i gyd a gawn
Bedeiroes mewn bedw iriawn.

❁ ❁ ❁

We'll talk to each other and it will be good,
We'll walk with each other through the wood.
We'll hug and stroke and court and all,
Our arms entwined, we'll be strong and hale.
I remember still how it felt, no strife or stress,
A lovely girl's neck with both hands to caress.
I'll build us a crystal chapel in rhyme
And a fragrant ointment I'll make sublime
And a comfy bed in a verdant dell
In a far off place, so all will be well.
We'll live a long time and in health we'll remain
Old age shall not wither us, nor mortal pain,
For we'll make a world from our true love
And live our lives in the lush birch grove.

We will talk to each other under the leaves,
We will walk together through woods and fresh foliage;
We will embrace, and court and all,
With our arms which will make us hale.
It was good work, without long misfortune,
To hold a girl's neck with two hands.
A glass chapel[1] from my verse
An ointment I myself will make,
And a bed in a green bush
A long way off, to prevent them finding our cover,
And to live long without spear or disease,
Without pain on us, without old age:
For we will have a good world together
Four lives in a fertile birch grove.[2]

---

1  *glass chapel*  The glass chapel is probably a reference to the glass house associated with Merlin in his role as a lover. It is also mentioned in the *cywydd* by Ieuan Dyfi "I Anni Goch" (see above).

2  *fertile birch grove*  The fertile birch grove is a stock setting in medieval Welsh love poetry where it is the setting for lovers' trysts. Cf. for example Dafydd ap Gwilym's *cywydd* "Y deildy" (The house of leaves). See http://www.dafyddapgwilym.net/eng/3win.htm

## 24. Cywydd i ofyn telyn rawn[1]

Gwerful wyf o gwr y llan,
O'r Fferi, lle hoff arian.
Cynnal arfer y Fferi
Tafarn ddifarn, ydd wyf i.
Cryswen lwys croesawa'n lan
Y gwŷr a ddaw ag arian,
Mynnwn fod, wrth gydfod gwŷr,
Fyd diwall i'm lletywyr,
A chanu yn lân gyfannedd
Yn eu mysg wrth lenwi medd.
Llanw yn hy, nid llawen hyn,
'Mysg tylwyth eisiau telyn.
Pan feddyliais, gwrtaisrodd,

※ ※ ※

## 24. Poem to ask for a harp

I'm Gwerful from the river bank,
The Ferry, where money's happy.
I keep up the Ferry's tradition,
It's a tavern open to everyone:
Clean white linen will welcome
The men who bring the handsome
Cash. I'll ensure my guests get their fill
And the company's crack will fit the bill,
Jubilant song will soar from below
While the mead cups overflow.
It fills up regular, and the only blot
Is it's lack of a harp—the company's not
Amused. When I pondered where I'd get

---

1 *Cywydd i ofyn telyn rawn*  There are four manuscript copies of this *cywydd*, to be found in the British Library, Cardiff Central Library, and the National Library of Wales.

# Gwerful ferch Gutun o Dalysarn, "Cywydd i ofyn telyn rawn"

This lively *cywydd*, with its female speaker who identifies herself as Gwerful, was long attributed to Gwerful Mechain, but recent scholarship has established that it is in fact the work of a later female poet, Gwerful ferch Gutun, who flourished in the mid sixteenth century. Nevertheless, the playful boldness of the voice and the poet's willingness to challenge and make demands of her male peers are certainly reminiscent of Gwerful Mechain, and suggest that she may be seen as an inspiration and literary mother to later Welsh women poets. The poem is a *cywydd gofyn* (a poem to ask for something), a traditional genre in medieval Welsh poetry, and the object requested, a harp, is also highly conventional. However, as Cathryn Charnell-White points out, Gwerful ferch Gutun's poem is much less obsequious in its praise of the patron than is often the case. See *Beirdd Ceridwen*, pp. 371–72.

## 24. Poem to ask for a harp

Gwerful am I from the corner of the riverside,
From the Ferry, money's favourite place.
Keeping up the customs of the Ferry,
A blameless tavern, am I.
A lovely white shirt gives a good welcome
To men who come with money,
I insist on being, with men's agreement,
Faultless to my guests,
And to sing sweetly and sociably
Among them as I replenish the mead.
Filling boldly, but this isn't jolly,
The company lacks a harp.
When I pondered, courteous gift,

Pe cawn delyn rawn o rodd,
Gyrrais gennad, rhoddiad rhydd,
I dŷ Ifan ap Dafydd,
Barwn yn rhoddi bara,
Barwniaid ei ddeudaid dda.
Mi a'i dygwn o waed agos,
Yn gâr i'r rhai gorau'n Rhos.
A'i geraint nis digarodd,
A'i gares wyf a gais rodd.
Ysto' rodd a'm gwnâi'n foddlawn,
Os da rhodd ag ystôr rhawn,
Ag ebillion ei llonaid
O'r cwr bwygilydd y'i caid,
A'r cweirgorn wrth ei chornel
A ddaw ple bynnag ydd êl,
A'i gwddw fal un o'r gwyddau,
A'r cefn yn ddigon cau.
Yno y'i caf am gywydd

A harp as a gift, I thought I'll bet
That Ifan ap Dafydd, an open-handed man,
Will come up trumps on this if anyone can,
So I sent a messenger to the baron's pad
He's baron of bread-giving, just like his grand-dad.
To tell you the truth, his blood is close to mine,
He's beloved of all the Rhos—the cool and fine;
His relatives he surely would not refuse,
And I'm his kinswoman, so I just can't lose.
Such a rare gift would make us all fair,
If it's packed in a case of soft horse hair,
And has pegs all along to serve us all,
Wherever it comes from, it'll grace a good hall.
Elegant as a goose's throat,
Its back curved like the keel of a boat.
I'm sure I'll get one for this verse:

How to get a horsehair-strung harp as a present,
I sent a messenger, free giving,
To Ifan ap Dafydd's[1] house,
Baron of giving bread,
Barons his two good grandfathers.
They are closely related by blood to me,
Beloved to the best of Rhos.
His relations he did not reject,
His kinswoman I am who's asking for a gift.
A generous gift would make me content,
If it's a good gift with a wealth of horsehair,
Full of pegs
From one end all the way to the other,
And the tuning fork at its corner
That comes wherever it goes,
And its neck like one of the geese,
And the back curved inwards enough.
There I will have it for a cywydd

---

1 *Ifan ap Dafydd* Ifan ap Dafydd seems to have been a local man living in the vicinity of Talysarn.

Yn rhodd, ac Ifan a'i rhydd.
Minnau roddaf i Ifan
Rost a medd os daw i'r man,
A'i groeso pan gano'r gog,
A'i ginio er dwy geiniog.

❀ ❀ ❀

Our Ifan will soon open up his purse.
Me, in return I'll give dear Ifan
A roast and mead if he comes to the tavern,
And a welcome when we hear the cuckoo,
And dinner, which costs a penny or two.

As a gift, and Ifan will give it.
I will give to Ifan
A roast and mead if he comes to this place,
And a welcome when the cuckoo sings,
And his dinner for two pennies.

## 25. Cywydd y gal

Rho Duw gal, rhaid yw gwyliaw
Arnad â llygad a llaw
Am hyn a hawl, pawl pensyth,
Yn amgenach bellach byth;
Rhwyd adain cont, rhaid ydiw
Rhag cwyn rhoi ffrwyn yn dy ffriw
I'th atal fal na'th dditier
Eilwaith, clyw anobaith clêr.
Casaf rholbren wyd gennyf,
Corn cod, na chyfod na chwyf;
Calennig gwragedd-da Cred,
Cylorffon ceuol arffed,
Ystum llindag, ceiliagwydd

## 25. Poem to the penis

By God, penis, I have to keep an eye on you
And keep you in hand—or we'll never come through.
Why? Oh you pole with your head held so high,
You've got us in trouble and the court case is nigh,
So it's better for now and for evermore
To bridle your snout—for you know the score:
You think you can catch every maiden in town
But stop—some of them will bring you down
And complain of your attentions once again.
So listen to me! Keep yourself in check
You despair of poets, you pain in the neck.
You vilest of rolling pins; big, swollen codpiece,
Bloated and thrusting: when will your antics cease?
You New Year's gift for the ladies of the world,
Nut tree growing in the lap's hollow curl,

# Dafydd ap Gwilym, "Cywydd y gal"[1]

Dafydd ap Gwilym (fl. c. 1315–c. 1370) was the best-known and most distinguished poet of medieval Wales. He came from northern Ceredigion, near Aberystwyth, but travelled the country as a bard, singing poems to his patrons. He is primarily a love poet and is often credited with establishing the *cywydd* as the most rich and flexible poetic form in the Welsh tradition. This humorous, erotic "Cywydd y gal/Poem to the penis" has been frequently misattributed to Gwerful Mechain; her "Cywydd y cedor/To the vagina" is believed to have been written as a riposte to this poem.

## 25. Poem to the penis

By God, penis, you've got to be guarded
Kept an eye and hand on,
For this reason, pole with head held high,
Better from now on and forever;
Net for a cunt's wing, it's necessary to
Bridle your snout to avoid complaint
To keep you in check so that you're not accused
Once again: listen to me, you despair of poets.
For me you're the vilest of rolling pins,
Horn of the codpiece, don't rise up or wave about;
New year's gift for the ladies of Christendom,
Nut stick of the lap's hollow,
Snare shape, gander,

---

1 *Cywydd y gal* There are 21 manuscript copies of this poem extant; interestingly, no fewer than five of them are attributed to Gwerful Mechain. The manuscripts are to be found in the University of Bangor, Cardiff Central Library, and the National Library of Wales.

Yn cysgu yn ei blu blwydd,
Paeled wlyb wddw paladflith,
Pen darn imp, paid â'th chwimp chwith;
Pyles gam, pawl ysgymun,
Piler bôn dau hanner bun,
Pen morlysywen den doll,
Pŵl argae fel pawl irgoll.
Hwy wyd na morddwyd mawrddyn,
Hirnos herwa, gannos gŷn;
Taradr fel paladr y post,
Benlledr a elwir bonllost.
Trosol wyd a bair traserch,
Clohigin clawr moeldin merch.
Chwibol yn dy siôl y sydd,
Chwibanogl gnuchio beunydd.
Y mae llygad i'th iaden
A wŷl pob gwreignith yn wen;

You snare, you gander, sleeping in soft down,
Neck with a wet shaft and milky white crown,
Tip of a shoot, stop your irritating twitching;
Bent one, damned pole, source of bitching;
You central pillar slicing a girl in half
You gimlet poking up like a flagstaff
You head of a conger eel with a narrow hole,
Blunt barrier like a sappy hazel bole.
You're longer than a big man's thigh,
An all-night hunter, always worth a try,
A chisel working hard for a hundred nights;
The eye in your head has a girl in its sights:
Every last girl in your eye is pretty
Every last girl's prey, more's the pity.
You leatherhead that's called a tail,
You're a club that beats out lust, without fail,
You're a peg for the lid on a girl's bare bottom
There's a wind-pipe in your column
A whistle for blowing, spring and autumn.

Sleeping in his yearling feathers,
Neck with a wet shaft and milky head,
Tip of a shoot, stop your irritating twitching;
Bent one, excommunicated pole,
Central pillar of the two halves of a girl,
Head of a conger eel with a narrow hole,
Blunt barrier like a sappy hazel branch.
You're longer than a big man's thigh,
A long night's pillage, a hundred nights' chisel;
A gimlet like the shaft of a post,
Leatherhead that's called a tail.
You're a club that causes lust,
A peg for the lid on a girl's bare bum.
There's a pipe in your shawl,
A whistle for fucking every day.
There's an eye in your head
That sees every girl as pretty;

Pestel crwn, gwn ar gynnydd,
Purdan ar gont fechan fydd;
Tobren arffed merchedau,
Tafod cloch yw'r tyfiad clau;
Cibyn dwl, ceibiai dylwyth,
Croen dagell, ffroen dwygaill ffrwyth.
Llodriad wyd o anlladrwydd,
Lledr d'wddw, llun asgwrn gwddw gŵydd;
Hwyl druth oll, hwl drythyllwg,
Hoel drws a bair hawl a drwg.
Ystyr fod gwrit a thitmant,
Ostwng dy ben, planbren plant.
Ys anodd dy gysoni,
Ysgwd oer, dioer gwae di!
Aml yw cerydd i'th unben,
Amlwg yw'r drwg drwy dy ben.

Curving pestle, you growing cannon grim,
You'll be purgatory for a small girl's quim;
You're a thatching-fork to trim a girl's bush,
Daft pod, you make families in a rush.
You're a bell's tongue that grows and falls;
You're the nose between two big fat balls.
Jowly skin round your shaft, like a goose's neck,
You doornail, cause of trouble and wreck,
You're a trouserful of lechery,
Deceitful, dishonest, a husk of debauchery.
Stop a minute, think, there's a writ on your head,
Abase yourself for once, you cad born and bred.
It's so hard to keep you under control,
Blast you, cold waterfall, blast you, blind pole!
You think you're in charge, though I often rebuke,
But the evil you do proves that you are no Duke.

Curved pestle, growing gun,
You'll be purgatory to a small cunt;
Thatching-fork of girls' laps,
A bell's tongue that grows so quick;
Daft pod, it dug a family,
Jowly skin, two fertile testicles' nose.
You're a trouserful of lechery,
Leatherneck, like a goose's neckbone;
Of deceitful nature, hull of debauchery,
Doornail that causes evil and trouble.
Just think, there's a writ and an indictment,
Lower your head, stick for planting offspring.
It's hard to keep you under control,
Cold waterfall, woe to you indeed!
Your lordship is often rebuked,
Evident is the evil done by you.

## 26. Englyn i'r gal[1]

Cal chwydlyd hyfryd yw hon—mwyn goflaid
    Mewn gaflau morynion;
    Sioba yn poeri sebon,
    Rhowter hers, rhad Duw ar hon.

❁ ❁ ❁

## 26. *Englyn* to the penis

A pretty cock throws up a lot—a sweet cwtsh
    In a maiden's crotch;
    A censer spitting soap froth,
    An arse router, God's grace be on't.

---

1   *Englyn i'r gal*   One copy of this anonymous englyn survives—in Peniarth 86, located in the National Library of Wales.

# Anonymous, "Englyn i'r gal"

This anonymous *englyn* is found in MS Peniarth 86. It has sometimes been attributed to Dafydd ap Gwilym and obviously bears some similarity to the latter's "Cywydd y gal" (above). Dafydd Johnston points out that the image of the censer (a container for sprinkling holy water) is also found in a poem by Dafydd ab Edmwnd (c. 1450–97) to Guto'r Glyn. See Johnston, *Canu maswedd yr oesoedd canol: Medieval Welsh erotic poetry.* It is a fond praise poem to the penis, displaying the poet's ingenuity in the *dyfalu*, in a brief space, of startling images.

## 26. *Englyn* to the penis

This is a pretty cock liable to vomiting—a nice embrace
    In a maiden's cleft;
  A censer spitting soapsuds,
  An arse beater, God's grace be on it.

# Bibliography

Charnell-White, Cathryn, "Alis, Catrin a Gwen: tair prydyddes o'r unfed ganrif ar bymtheg. Tair chwaer?," *Dwned: Cylchgrawn Hanes a Llên Cymru'r Oesoedd Canol* V (1999): 89–104. ["Alis, Catrin and Gwen: three female poets of the sixteenth century. Three sisters?", *Dwned: Journal of the History and Literature of the Middle Ages*]

Charnell-White, Cathryn, ed., *Beirdd Ceridwen: Blodeugerdd Barddas o Ganu Menywod hyd tua 1800*, Llandybïe: Barddas, 2005. [*Ceridwen's poets: the Barddas Anthology of Women's Verse up to c. 1800*]

Charnell-White, Cathryn, "Barddoniaeth ddefosiynol Catrin ferch Gruffudd ap Hywel," *Dwned* 7 (2001): 93–120. [The devotional poetry of Catrin daughter of Gruffudd ap Hywel]

Charnell-White, Cathryn, "Problems of Authorship and Attribution: The Welsh-Language Women's Canon before 1800," *Women's Writing* (2017), pp. 1–20.

Clancy, Joseph, *Medieval Welsh Poems*, Dublin: Four Courts, 2002.

Curtis, Kathryn, "Beirdd benywaidd yng Nghymru cyn 1800," *Y Traethodydd* vol. CXLI 598 (1986): 12–27. [Female poets in Wales before 1800, *The Essayist*]

Dafydd ap Gwilym online: http://www.dafyddapgwilym.net.

*Geiriadur Prifysgol Cymru* arlein/online, available at http://geiriadur.ac.uk/gpc/gpc.html. [*The University of Wales Dictionary online*]

Greer, Germaine, *Slip-shod Sibyls: Recognition, Rejection and the Woman Poet*, London: Viking Penguin, 1995.

Gruffydd, W.J., *Llenyddiaeth Cymru o 1450 hyd 1600*, Liverpool: Hugh Evans and Sons, 1922. [*The Literature of Wales from 1450 to 1600*]

Harries, Leslie, *Barddoniaeth Huw Cae Llwyd, Ieuan Dyfi, a Gwerful Mechain*, M.A. Thesis, University of Wales, 1933. [*The Poetry of Huw Cae Llwyd, Ieuan Dyfi, and Gwerful Mechain*]

Haycock, Marged, "Merched Drwg a Merched Da: Ieuan Dyfi v. Gwerful Mechain," *Ysgrifau Beirniadol* XVI (1990): 97–110. ["Bad Women and Good Women: Ieuan Dyfi v. Gwerful Mechain," *Critical Essays*]

Haycock, Marged, "'Defnydd hyd Ddydd Brawd': Rhai Agweddau ar y Ferch ym Marddoniaeth yr Oesoedd Canol." In *Wales and the Welsh 2000/Cymru a'r Cymry 2000*, ed., Geraint H. Jenkins, Aberystwyth: University of Wales Centre for Advanced Welsh and Celtic Studies, 2001, pp. 41–70. ["Material until Judgement Day": Some Aspects of Women in Medieval Poetry]

Haycock, Marged, "Dwsin o brydyddesau? Achos Gwladus 'Hael' ac eraill," *Dwned: Cylchgrawn Hanes a Llên Cymru'r Oesoedd Canol* 16 (2010): 93–114. ["A Dozen Poetesses? The case of 'Generous' Gwladys and others"]

Howells, Nerys Ann, ed., *Gwaith Gwerful Mechain ac Eraill*, Aberystwyth: Canolfan Uwchefrydiau Cymreig a Cheltaidd, 2001. [*The Work of Gwerful Mechain and others*, Aberystwyth: Centre for Advanced Welsh and Celtic Studies]

Jenkins, Nia Mai, "'A'i gyrfa megis Gwerful': Bywyd a Gwaith Angharad James," *Llên Cymru* 24 (1997): 79–112. ["And her career like Gwerful's": The Life and Work of Angharad James, *The Literature of Wales*]

Johnston, Dafydd, "The Erotic Poetry of the *Cywyddwyr*," *Cambridge Medieval Celtic Studies* 22 (1991): 63–94.

Johnston, Dafydd, ed., *Canu maswedd yr oesoedd canol: Medieval Welsh erotic poetry*, Cardiff: Tafol, 1991.

Johnston, Dafydd, "Gwenllian ferch Rhirid Flaidd," *Dwned* III (1997): 27–32. [Gwenllian the daughter of Rhirid Flaidd]

Jones, Gwen Saunders, *Alis ferch Gruffudd a'r Traddodiad Barddol Benywaidd*, Caernarfon: Gwasg Pantycelyn, 2015. [*Alis the daughter of Gruffudd and the Female Bardic Tradition*]

Lloyd, Margaret, "Gwerful Mechain (c. 1462–1500)," *Poetry Wales* 29 (April, 1994): 42–45.

Lloyd-Morgan, Ceridwen, "'Gwerful, ferch ragorol fain': Golwg Newydd ar Gwerful Mechain," *Ysgrifau Beirniadol* XVI (1990): 84–96. ["'Gwerful, excellent slim daughter': A New View of Gwerful Mechain," *Critical Essays*]

Lloyd-Morgan, Ceridwen, "Women and their poetry in medieval Wales." In *Women and Literature in Britain, 1150–1500*, ed. Carol M. Meale, Cambridge University Press, 1993, pp. 183–201.

Lloyd-Morgan, Ceridwen, "The 'Querelle des Femmes': A Continuing Tradition in Welsh Women's Literature." In *Medieval Women: Texts and Contexts in Late Medieval Britain: Essays for Felicity Riddy*, eds. Jocelyn Wogan-Browne et al., Turnhout: Brepols, 2000, pp. 101–14.

Lloyd-Morgan, Ceridwen, "Oral Composition and Written Transmission: Welsh Women's Poetry from the Middle Ages and Beyond," *Trivium* XXVI (1991): 89–102.

Lloyd-Morgan, Ceridwen and Kathryn Hughes, *Telyn Egryn*, Dinas Powys: Honno, 1998. [*The Harp of Egryn*]

Mackay, Peter and Iain S. MacPherson, eds., *An Leabhar Liath/The Light Blue Book: Five Hundred Years of Gaelic Love and Transgressive Verse*, Edinburgh: Luath Press, 2017.

*Mynegai i Farddoniaeth Gaeth y Llawysgrifau (Index to the Strict Metre Poetry in the Manuscripts)*. [Index to the Strict Metre Poetry in the Manuscripts]

Powell, Nia, "Women and Strict-Metre Poetry in Wales." In *Women and Gender in Early Modern Wales*, eds. Michael Roberts and Simone Clarke, Cardiff: University of Wales Press, 2000, pp. 129–58.

Roberts, Enid, *Dafydd Llwyd o Fathafarn*, Darlith Lenyddol Eisteddfod Genedlaethol Cymru, Maldwyn a'r Cyffiniau, 1981. [*Dafydd Llwyd of Mathafarn*, The Literary Lecture of the National Eisteddfod of Wales, Maldwyn and region]

Smith, Llinos Beverley, "Olrhain Anni Goch," *Ysgrifau Beirniadol* XIX (1993): 107–26. [Tracing Red Annie, *Critical Essays*]

Stephens, Meic, ed., *The New Companion to the Literature of Wales*, Cardiff: University of Wales Press, 1998.

Watt, Diane, ed., *Medieval Women in Their Communities*, Cardiff: University of Wales Press, 1997.

Williams, Glanmor, "Religion and Welsh Literature in the Age of the Reformation," *Proceedings of the British Academy* 69 (1983): 371–408.

Williams, Glanmor, *Recovery, Reorientation, and Reformation: Wales c. 1415–1642*, Oxford: Oxford University Press, 1993.

## From the Publisher

A name never says it all, but the word "Broadview" expresses a
good deal of the philosophy behind our company. We are open to
a broad range of academic approaches and political viewpoints.
We pay attention to the broad impact book publishing and book
printing has in the wider world; for some years now we have used
100% recycled paper for most titles. Our publishing program is
internationally oriented and broad-ranging. Our individual titles
often appeal to a broad readership too; many are of interest as
much to general readers as to academics and students.

Founded in 1985, Broadview remains a fully independent
company owned by its shareholders—not an imprint
or subsidiary of a larger multinational.

For the most accurate information on our books
(including information on pricing, editions, and formats)
please visit our website at www.broadviewpress.com.
Our print books and ebooks are also available for sale on our site.

broadview press
www.broadviewpress.com

The interior of this book is printed on 100% recycled paper.

PERMANENT 100%